"What are you doing here?"

Emma turned her head to meet the full force of Lord Brandford's cold and angry stare. She smiled politely.

"I came to offer my sincerest apologies for having inconvenienced you."

"Inconvenienced!" bellowed Lord Brandford. "You hoyden!"

Emma did not appreciate his description. She stood up and glared at him. "It is all your fault!"

"All *my* fault?" gasped Lord Brandford.

"Certainly," explained Emma. "If you hadn't shouted at me, nothing would have gone amiss. I have slid down the bannisters here countless times before and nobody has been the wiser."

"If I hadn't..." spluttered the lord. "You scapegrace! You hussy! You... you..."

Emma surveyed him primly. In a perfect imitation of her Headmistresses at their most disparaging she announced, "I withdraw my apology. You are unworthy of it. Instead," she concluded, "I think you should apologize to me."

At that precise moment, in came the Headmistress and Emma was spared Lord Brandford's own unique idea of an apology.

Books by Blanche Chenier

HARLEQUIN REGENCY ROMANCE
19–LUCINDA

THE WAYWARD HEIRESS

BLANCHE CHENIER

Harlequin Books

TORONTO • NEW YORK • LONDON
AMSTERDAM • PARIS • SYDNEY • HAMBURG
STOCKHOLM • ATHENS • TOKYO • MILAN

Published November 1990

ISBN 0-373-31137-0

Printed in U.S.A.

CHAPTER ONE

"EMMA!" INTONED Miss Foxall in what Emma had come to think of as her Doomsday voice. "I should be obliged if you would pick yourself up, go to the study and wait for me there."

Emma worried her lower lip with her pretty white teeth, hoping she looked suitably contrite.

"I am frightfully sorry, Miss Foxall."

Emma was bruised, particularly on her derriere. She hauled herself up from the polished marble floor by means of the bannister—that same bannister which had been her downfall.

Emma's unintended victim was rubbing her ankle, surrounded by a score of Emma's fellow pupils, who were making sympathetic noises and offering helpful suggestions.

Emma folded her hands demurely in front of her and approached, saying, "I am most awfully sorry."

The other young lady's limpid brown eyes were brimming with tears. She glanced momentarily at Emma and seemed about to speak; however, any words she was going to say were immediately cut short by the enraged gentleman at her side.

Bristling with fury, he rounded on Emma. "So you should be! If you were my daughter..."

Miss Foxall coughed. It was a soft cough, but one which had taken years of practise to perfect, and it had the effect of silencing the gentleman immediately.

"Lord Brandford," said Miss Foxall, "*I* shall deal with the matter."

Lord Brandford bit back his anger, and Emma retired.

EXPERIENCE HAD TAUGHT EMMA to knock timidly on the door labelled Miss Foxall. Miss Quince. Study. before entering.

"Come in!" called Miss Quince in answer to her light rap.

As Emma entered the Inner Sanctum, Miss Quince's welcoming smile wavered. "Good afternoon, Emma."

"Good afternoon, Miss Quince." Emma replied, dropping a curtsy. "Miss Foxall asked me to wait here."

"I see."

Emma, head bowed, took a seat on a straight-backed chair opposite her and with her hands resting in her lap, waited patiently.

A few moments later, Miss Foxall herself entered the study and seated herself beside her partner, Miss Quince. Both ladies turned severe and disapproving gazes upon their pupil.

"Emma," observed Miss Foxall, "the bannisters at the Houghton Academy for Young Ladies are *not* for sliding down."

"No, Miss Foxall," replied Emma meekly. "I'm sorry, Miss Foxall."

"I sincerely hope and trust that you will not be tempted to descend by that method again."

"No, Miss Foxall."

"You have by your rashness not only injured a perfectly innocent bystander..."

Emma's eyes flashed indignantly. She was about to deny it, but realized in the nick of time that such a course would not endear her to the two Headmistresses.

"But, furthermore," continued Miss Foxall grimly, "you have very probably robbed the Academy of a new pupil."

Emma gasped. "Oh dear! I *am* sorry, Miss Foxall!" This time she meant it.

"I am sure you are, Emma." Miss Foxall sighed deeply. "I suggest that the first thing you can do to try to repair the damage is to apologize to Lady Marcella Brandford. You will find her in the front drawing room. Kindly have the goodness to wait until after the doctor has seen to her ankle."

"Yes, Miss Foxall."

"You will then attend upon Lady Marcella while Lord Brandford goes into Houghton Regina to arrange for a suitable conveyance to drive them back to London."

"Yes, Miss Foxall. I'm sorry, Miss Foxall." As she received the sign of dismissal, Emma curtsied once more. "Thank you, Miss Foxall. Thank you, Miss Quince."

One always said "thank you" to Miss Foxall and Miss Quince—even if one were being scolded, and even if by some remote chance the rebuke was unjust. It was considered that thanks were still due to the Headmistresses for the trouble they took to instruct one.

EMMA SMOOTHED the long white linen apron which formed a part of the Academy uniform. Her golden curls were tied with a ribbon. She fluffed the royal-blue sleeve of her merino gown and twirled round to ensure that the skirt hung straight.

When she was presentable, Emma knocked upon the door of the front drawing room and on being invited, entered.

Lady Marcella Brandford was stretched out upon the green tapestried chaise longue with her bandaged foot placed on a pink velvet cushion. Her brown riding habit fell to the floor.

As Emma closed the door behind her, Lady Marcella glanced at her visitor.

Emma curtsied.

Lady Marcella inclined her head in acknowledgement.

"I have come," began Emma, "to apologize for my disgraceful conduct—"

"Apologize?" interrupted Lady Marcella. "Oh, pray do not apologize! I could not be more pleased!"

"Pleased?" Emma's angelic-blue eyes were as round as saucers.

"Certainly." Lady Marcella's cheeks were flushed with excitement. "I didn't want to come here, you see. And now I shan't have to. It's wonderful! It couldn't have worked out better! I am in your debt! Oh, do please sit down and let us be friends."

As if in a dream, Emma crossed the luxurious carpet. She lowered herself into a Sheraton chair. "I—I don't understand."

Lady Marcella stared at her as if the notion had only just occurred to her. "Oh! No, I suppose you don't." She smiled suddenly. "Well, you see, it's like this. I'm in love."

Emma moved closer and listened attentively.

"He is absolutely divine, a perfect gentleman, and the perfect husband for me." Lady Marcella frowned. "The only trouble is Charles."

"Charles?"

"My brother. You met him out there."

Emma pursed her lips. She recollected only too clearly the tall Corinthian with his windswept brown hair, his elegantly chiselled features, and his brown eyes smouldering like a peat fire.

"Charles," continued Lady Marcella, "is inclined to be a little overbearing at times."

Emma's eyebrows arched. "He seems to have . . . a quick temper."

"You mustn't take any notice of that. I never do. At least," she amended, "not if I can help it."

Emma put her hand in front of her mouth to smother a giggle.

"We shall be friends, shan't we?" urged Lady Marcella.

"Oh, yes. I should like nothing better."

"Good. Then you shall call me Marcella. And you are...?"

"Emma."

Lady Marcella leaned forward. In a low whisper she went on. "The trouble is that Charles is ten years older than I. He tends to look upon me as a little girl of seven. But I am not seven, I am seventeen, and I know my own mind. In spite of what Charles thinks, I know Louis is the right man for me."

"Louis?"

"Louis de Troyes. My fiancé."

"Oh." Emma considered. "He is French?"

"Yes. But only by the merest chance. He was born in Languedoc, you see. But before he was a year old, the Bastille had fallen and his parents fled to Bohemia. Then, during the Peace of Amiens, they came to England, and they have been here ever since."

Emma frowned. "Why didn't they return to France during the Peace?"

"Louis's father would have nothing to do with the Corsican ogre!"

"Hmm." So Louis de Troyes was presumably as opposed to Napoleon as any Englishman would be. "What do your parents think?"

Lady Marcella sighed heartrendingly. "Father dear died two years ago, at Talavera..."

"Oh, did he? That is a shame. My father died then, too."

"Really? I am sorry. Who was your father?"

"George Armstead, er, Colonel Armstead," she amended.

"Umm. My father was the Eighth Earl of Brandford. Charles is the Ninth Earl." She thought for a moment. "No.

I don't believe I have heard of a Colonel Armstead. But it was a very big battle."

Emma nodded in agreement.

"If Father dear were alive, I should probably have had his consent to marry Louis. And Mother dear probably would have said yes if Charles hadn't gone on about how young I am." Lady Marcella grimaced. "He persuaded her to pack me off here until I am 'a little older.'" She mimicked him disdainfully. "He behaved for all the world as if my wanting to marry Louis were some kind of childhood ailment, like chicken pox or the mumps."

Emma laughed.

"You understand?" demanded Lady Marcella. "Charles cannot keep me here now because I have injured my ankle. Miss Quince and Miss Foxall are sure to inform Mother dear. And once Mother dear knows, she will fret. Charles promised Father dear that he would never allow anyone to distress Mother dear. So we must return to London." She sighed ecstatically. "And Louis..." She clasped Emma's hands and pressed them fervently. "Do you see why I am so grateful to you?"

"Yes. But—" Emma did not get any further.

At that moment the door opened and Lady Marcella's brother came in.

Lady Marcella threw herself back on the cushions with a groan, achieving a martyred air which would have done credit to a saint.

Emma turned her head to meet the full force of Lord Brandford's cold and angry stare.

"What are *you* doing in here?"

Emma smiled politely. "I came to offer my sincerest apologies to your poor, dear sister. She has been gracious enough to accept them."

"Has she, indeed!" hissed the earl.

"I also regret having inconvenienced you."

"Inconvenienced! You hoyden!"

The apologetic smile left Emma's face. She stiffened.

"Have you any idea of the damage you have done?" growled Lord Brandford. "My sister is prostrate. And what our poor mother will say when she hears of this incident I cannot imagine. We did not expect, when we came to the Houghton Academy for Young Ladies, to find it in the hands of a horde of Amazons."

Emma did not appreciate his description. She stood up and glared at him. "It is all your fault!"

Lady Marcella's eyes flew open in astonishment.

"All *my* fault?" gasped Lord Brandford.

"Certainly. If you hadn't shouted at me, nothing would have gone amiss. It is entirely your fault."

"You . . . you . . ."

"I have slid down the bannisters here countless times before and nobody has been the wiser." Emma turned to Lady Marcella. "It is great fun. You ought to try it, when you are better."

Lord Brandford's hands clenched at his sides. "How dare you tell my sister—"

His exclamation was cut short as Emma continued. "Marcella could have . . ."

"Marcella?"

"Your sister has given me her kind permission to call her by her Christian name, without the title attached. It was very good of her. She shows a most forgiving spirit—unlike some I could name."

"Why you . . . !"

Emma was undeterred by his fury. "As I was saying, Marcella could have moved out of the way. But you had to start shouting, in a most unseemly way. I am not surprised she froze, for I myself lost concentration. I was so taken aback that instead of drawing my legs in at the corner as I usually do, I left them sticking out, which is why poor

Marcella was accidentally kicked and fell, twisting her ankle. So you see, it is entirely your fault—if you hadn't barked like a mad dog, nothing would have happened."

"If I hadn't..." spluttered Lord Brandford. "You scapegrace! You hussy! You...you..."

Emma surveyed him primly. In a perfect imitation of her Headmistresses at their most disparaging, she announced, "I withdraw my apology. You are too unworthy of it."

Lord Brandford ground his teeth.

"Instead," concluded Emma, "I think you should apologize to us."

Lady Marcella whipped out a handkerchief with her monogram in one corner and made some small choking noises into it.

Lord Brandford's brown eyes were almost popping out of his head. His lips parted into what promised to be a snarl.

It was at that moment Miss Quince entered the room.

CHAPTER TWO

"LORD BRANDFORD, Lady Marcella." Miss Quince smiled sweetly. With her grey hair and in her magenta gown, she looked exactly like a favourite aunt. "I understand you have been unable to find a satisfactory conveyance in Houghton Regina. Miss Foxall and I naturally thought we should offer you accommodation here until Lady Marcella's ankle is healed."

"Thank you!" replied Lady Marcella. "That is very generous of you."

"No!" exploded Lord Brandford. "We cannot accept!"

Miss Quince blinked. Her light grey eyes darted nervously across the room to Emma, who was moving slowly towards the window. "Oh, I am sorry." And then, beguilingly, "Miss Foxall and I had been rather looking forward to the pleasure of your company."

Lady Marcella favoured the Headmistress with an angelic smile. She had no chance to speak, however.

Lord Brandford, breathing fire, declared, "That person has insulted us." His black-gloved hand extended towards Emma.

Miss Quince looked suitably astonished. "Miss Armstead has insulted you?"

"Yes!" His tone implied that it was impossible for him or his sister to stay under the same roof with a female who had besmirched their honour.

Emma was innocence personified. "I am so sorry, Lord Brandford. I had no idea that I had been rude. I do offer you my most humble apologies.'' She emphasized her sincere contrition with a graceful curtsey.

Lord Brandford kicked a lump of coal back into the fire. His glossy dark-leather boots reflected the glow of the flames. ''I do not think a simple apology will do.''

Lady Marcella sat bolt upright. ''Oh, Charles, don't be a bore. He is only cross, Miss Quince, because Emma stood up to him.''

Miss Quince's fine grey eyebrows arched. The use of her pupil's Christian name did not escape her.

Lord Brandford's countenance was almost the same colour as his sable riding coat. ''I'll thank you to keep out of this, Marcella!''

''I won't keep out of it!'' countered his sister. ''Emma was trying to apologize to you and you were most ungracious. I'm not surprised she withdrew her apology.''

''Marcella, I'm warning you . . .''

Lady Marcella reclined once more. She had scarcely settled into her noble-martyr pose when again the door of the drawing room opened wide. This time Miss Foxall entered.

''I heard raised voices. Is anything the matter?''

A guilty silence fell.

Emma had shifted even closer to the window. She peered out across the snow-covered lawns. By the gate, she could see a man, hovering.

When no one else spoke, Miss Quince remarked, ''Lord Brandford feels unable to accept our hospitality, Miss Foxall.''

''Indeed?'' Miss Foxall turned her unnerving gaze upon the earl. ''Why?''

Lord Brandford was taken aback by the Headmistress's directness. ''I, er, feel that the atmosphere of your school would be, ahem, inappropriate for my sister.''

''Really?''

"Your, um, pupil over there...I have forgotten her name—" with a flick of his ruffled sleeve he indicated Emma "—has insulted us."

Lady Marcella looked as if she were about to protest, but a glance from her brother made her change her mind.

Miss Foxall pursed her lips. "I am sure Miss Armstead would never be *intentionally* rude, and I am equally sure that if you pointed out her error, she would apologize for it."

"She has already done so," said Miss Quince.

"I see." Miss Foxall's piercing eyes fastened once again upon Lord Brandford. "I do hope you can find it in your heart as a Christian to accept Miss Armstead's apologies."

"Naturally, I accept." Lord Brandford sounded anything but mollified. "However, I do not feel that I can allow my sister to remain here. Experience has shown that at your Academy, she is likely to be abused or injured at every turn...."

"You exaggerate," cut in Miss Foxall. "Our Academy is a school for young ladies, not young barbarians. In any case, your sister is in no condition to ride back to London."

"Nonsense! She is perfectly capable of it."

"I think not." Miss Foxall's clipped tones did not encourage opposition.

"Oh, I quite agree," murmured Miss Quince. "Lady Marcella's foot is rather badly swollen. It would be another matter if a carriage were available. But if she were to ride, goodness knows what damage would be done. We must consider her future, Lord Brandford."

Fiery sparks shot from the earl's brown eyes. "I am doing just that!" He turned, seething, to his sister. "Marcella, you will prepare to leave here within the next half hour. I should be obliged to you, Miss Foxall, if you would give the order for our horses to be saddled."

"I beg your pardon, Lord Brandford, but you may *not* have any horses." Miss Foxall's tone was level and quiet. She might have been reading out a laundry list for all the emotion she displayed. "We cannot allow Lady Marcella to travel in her present condition. Since there is no suitable conveyance, it is imperative that she remain here." Miss Foxall allowed a smile to appear. "You are our guests, Lady Marcella, Lord Brandford. Please feel free to make use of every facility our Academy has to offer. We are at your disposal."

Miss Foxall made a slight curtsey. Miss Quince followed suit. Then both Headmistresses departed.

Lord Brandford, caught off balance, watched them mutely. Suddenly he found his voice and charged after the Headmistresses, shouting, "Just a minute..."

As the door closed behind him, Emma left the window. She came over to Lady Marcella's side.

"Tell me, your Louis de Troyes, is he by any chance rather slender and fair?"

"Yes! How did you know?"

"There is a slender and fair man standing uncertainly by the gate, as if he is waiting for someone, and since he is not from Houghton Regina..."

Lady Marcella clapped her hands joyfully. "Oh, the darling! He has travelled all the way up here to be near me! He has not counted the cost! Oh, my poor lamb!" Confidently, she addressed Emma. "He is not a wealthy man. He must have starved for a week to find the money! And just for me!" A frown crossed her features. "Poor Louis! He'll freeze to death if he is left out there in the cold! Emma dearest, might you send him a note for me?"

"Of course." A wicked smile played about Emma's lips. "It is *my* duty tonight to close the gates, as soon as the sun sets."

WRAPPED IN A WARM fur-lined pelisse, Emma walked down the frozen path to the gate. Her gloved hands rested upon the wrought ironwork. "Monsieur de Troyes?"

He appeared from behind the gatepost and bowed. "I am Louis de Troyes. You have a message for me?"

Emma handed him Lady Marcella's letter. He seized it fervently and kissed it passionately.

Emma watched him dreamily, recalling Lady Marcella's words. "Our lawyer—such a stuffy fellow—was convinced dearest Louis was a fortune-hunter. He told Louis that under the terms of Father dear's will I would inherit nothing if I married him. He expected Louis to withdraw his proposal, but, bless him, he did not."

Oh, if only there were someone, thought Emma, *who loved me for myself alone!*

"OH, YOU TWO KNOW each other!" Miss Quince was rapturous. "Then there is no need for me to introduce you."

Lord Brandford bowed deeply to Louis de Troyes.

Despite Miss Quince's best efforts, he had still not recovered his good humour. Miss Foxall and Miss Quince had made him feel vaguely guilty, just as his nanny had done once when he was a little boy of four and had eaten too many jam tarts. He resented it, and his temper was about to flare, when he remembered his surroundings.

The dining hall of the Houghton Academy for Young Ladies was not the place for a gentleman to give vent to his frustration.

Already the pupils were filing in, filling table after beechwood table. Curious eyes were turning in his direction and—he could not forebear shuddering—some of the younger girls were actually snickering!

"Pray be seated, Lord Brandford, Mr. de Troyes," invited Miss Foxall.

The Headmistresses' table was upon a dais at one end of the dining hall. From it, Miss Foxall and Miss Quince were able to survey their charges and to ensure that they kept out of mischief.

Lord Brandford registered the fact that the pupils wore uniforms, whereas the staff did not.

There was a mass scraping of chairs as the ladies seated themselves. Lord Brandford and Louis de Troyes, too, took their places.

"You look worried, Lord Brandford," stated Miss Foxall.

"I was puzzled . . . how does Mr. de Troyes come to be here?"

"He lost his way in the snow and came across our school. It is easy to see, being situated on a hill. At night, it is always ablaze with lights, and I am told it is a landmark for travellers in this part of Wiltshire."

"Of course," Miss Quince adjusted the brooch pinned to her ginger cashmere gown, "we admitted him, and he will stay until morning."

"I notice you have no male staff," observed Lord Brandford dryly.

"It would be inadvisable."

"Yet you are willing to take in stray travellers. . . ."

"A gentleman of your acquaintance," noted Miss Foxall, "can hardly be considered a stray traveller."

Lady Marcella smothered a laugh.

Lord Brandford glowered at her.

"Although we are an Academy for young ladies," added Miss Quince, "we do admit gentlemen on occasion, if the necessity arises. Usually such gentlemen are the fathers or brothers of our pupils. Sometimes, as tonight, they are friends of the family."

Miss Foxall arranged her silver shawl. "It is quite impossible for such visitors to sleep in Houghton Hall itself. That is why it is so fortunate that you two know each other. You may, therefore, enjoy each other's company in Houghton Lodge.''

Lord Brandford looked as if he would have liked to throttle Miss Foxall. ''And my sister?''

''Lady Marcella will be housed with Miss Armstead, who, I am sure, will attend to her needs,'' Miss Quince informed him.

Lord Brandford's knife and fork were clenched so tightly in his hands that Miss Quince began to fear he would snap the bone handles.

''May I ask how you arrived at this decision?''

''Certainly,'' answered Miss Foxall. ''Miss Armstead is the senior girl in this establishment. She is nineteen years old, two years older than your sister. She has the authority and the capacity to care for her.''

Louis de Troyes frowned. For the first time since they had been seated, he ventured to speak. ''Forgive me, Miss Foxall, but I seem to remember someone telling me that you took young ladies between the ages of twelve and eighteen.''

''Those are our rules. However, one sometimes has to make exceptions.''

''Of course.'' His gaze travelled to Lady Marcella. A look of tenderness passed between them.

Miss Foxall and Miss Quince, alert to the ways of young ladies, noticed immediately. They exchanged glances. There was no need to say a word.

MISS QUINCE SIPPED a hot milk-and-honey posset. ''We are going to have to do something about Emma.''

''Why?'' demanded Miss Foxall. ''Is she ill?''

''She needs a husband.''

Miss Foxall eyed her partner balefully. ''What do you suggest that we do about it, Naomi? Put an advertisement in the *Houghton Clarion*, perhaps? 'Charming but slightly wayward heiress requires suitable spouse?''

"Artemisia," answered Miss Quince rebukingly, "it is hardly a laughing matter.''

Miss Foxall shrugged and pulled her silver shawl closer about her.

"Emma," continued Miss Quince, "as you reminded me at dinner, is nineteen years old. In less than six months, she will be twenty. We really cannot keep her at the Academy much longer.''

Miss Foxall plucked the poker from its bronze stand and stirred the log fire into a roaring blaze. "We can't send her away. She has no relations, and if she enters Society, wealthy as she is, with no one to protect her, heaven only knows what will happen!''

Miss Quince put down her cup. She went to ensure that the nut-brown shutters were secure, then seated herself before the fire once more and nursed her posset in her hands.

"I had rather hoped that one of the other girls would invite Emma to stay. She could then have been launched into Society by somebody's mama.''

Miss Foxall pricked up her ears at a noise outside their private sitting room.

The young ladies of the Academy were, on occasion, inclined to eavesdrop. Miss Foxall yanked the door open. There was not a pupil in sight.

The noise had been caused by one of the staff, who had been carrying too large a pile of textbooks and had dropped every single one of them a little distance away. Now, red-faced with embarrassment, she was hurriedly retrieving them.

Miss Foxall decided not to add to her agonies by offering to help. She closed the sitting-room door and locked it.

"It is most unfortunate that has not come to pass. The friends Emma has made do not move in the upper echelons of Society."

Miss Quince nodded forlornly. Emma's friends were reasonably comfortable, but far from wealthy. "I doubt if any of them realize the extent of Emma's fortune."

"It is just as well they don't!"

"Quite." She paused. "I was rather hoping the Dowager Countess of Brandford might be induced to do the job."

"If I were Lady Brandford, I would do no such thing! Have you seen how hostile the earl is towards Emma?"

"I had noticed he got a bit carried away."

"Carried away? My dear Naomi, what do you mean?"

Miss Quince smiled gently. "The young can be so violent in their passions, Artemisia. It is not always easy for them to distinguish love from hate, or rage from desire."

Miss Foxall considered the matter. She poured some brandy into her own hot posset. "Of course, one might point out to Lady Brandford that if Emma and Lady Marcella were constantly together, it would make things, ahem, difficult for any fortune hunter."

"Such as Louis de Troyes?"

"If he *is* a fortune hunter, which I doubt."

"Oh, do you? Upon what evidence?"

"His manner towards Lady Marcella. That kind of tenderness cannot be feigned."

"Hmm. I daresay you are right." Miss Quince half closed her grey eyes. "Will you write to Lady Brandford or shall I?"

"You do it, Naomi. You are so much better at these things." Miss Foxall yawned. "I am tired. I shall go to bed now. Good night." She directed her steps to a door at the left of the sitting room.

"Good night, Artemisia."

Miss Quince remained in solitary thought for several minutes. Then she finished her posset and placed the empty cup on the tray beside her partner's.

Comfortably ensconced at the mahogany writing desk, Miss Quince opened the pewter ink well. She dipped in the best of her quills and composed a refined letter to Lady Brandford.

That task completed, Miss Quince sprinkled salt lightly over the ink to dry it, folded the missive and sealed it with her personal seal before retiring to her own bedroom on the right of the sitting room.

CHAPTER THREE

"MOTHER DEAR!" The appearance of Lady Brandford in his sister's rooms took the earl by surprise.

Her ladyship had already greeted her daughter. Now she tilted her head so that her son could kiss her cheek without colliding with her ultramarine velvet Spanish hat. "Charles." Her brown eyes widened suddenly. "What have you got on your feet?"

"Skates, Mother dear." He was thankful for the wooden protectors on the blades. They spared him a lengthy dissertation upon the proper care of floors.

"You have been out on the ice? I do hope you have not caught cold!"

"I was too energetic to catch cold."

"I am so glad." She smiled warmly at her son and at his companion. "Dear Louis!"

"Lady Brandford." Louis de Troyes bowed and kissed her fingertips. "I hope you had a good journey?"

"Most pleasant, considering the state of the roads at this time of year, thank you." She gazed accusingly at her son. "I had no idea Houghton Regina was so far from London! You did not tell me, Charles, that you were sending Marcella into the wilderness!"

Lord Brandford's mouth tightened. "Houghton Regina is *not* in the wilderness, Mother dear. It is scarcely twenty miles from Salisbury. In any case, Marcella is not staying...."

"No, of course she isn't. She is returning to London with us."

"Us?" questioned Lord Brandford suspiciously.

"Yes, Charles. You and I and Louis—and dear Miss Armstead."

Louis de Troyes only just managed to smother a cry of astonishment mingled with alarm.

It was at that moment that Emma reentered the room, carrying a large woollen rug which she placed over Lady Marcella's legs. "There you are. Better?"

"Yes, thank you."

"I, er, beg your pardon?" Lord Brandford's tones were dangerously soft. "I didn't quite catch..."

"Emma is coming with us to London!" exclaimed Lady Marcella. "Isn't it wonderful?"

Lord Brandford stared at his mother and sister in horror and disbelief.

Emma smiled winsomely at him. "We are going to have such fun together, Marcella and I." Then she addressed Lady Brandford. "I am really very grateful to you for your invitation."

Lord Brandford was speechless.

"Excuse me." Louis de Troyes retreated, bowing. "I must change. I fell on the ice, and my clothes are a trifle damp."

Lord Brandford found his voice. "Mother dear, might I have a word with you?"

"Certainly."

"In private."

Lady Brandford shrugged her shoulders. Her topaz satin pelisse rustled with the movement. "I don't know whether there is anywhere where we may be private. This is a school, not—"

"There is the front drawing room," suggested Emma. "I'll take you there, if you like."

LADY BRANDFORD CHOSE the same leaf-tapestried chaise longue where her daughter had lain after her accident. "Now, what is the matter, Charles?"

The Earl of Brandford waited until the door was tightly shut. Then, his every word vibrating with passion, he answered, "Your invitation to Miss Armstead is ill-advised."

"Charles, don't be disagreeable. She is a charming young lady. Marcella likes her, Louis likes her, and I mean to have her as my guest."

"Over my dead body!"

Lady Brandford's hand went up to her forehead. "You are being beastly, Charles. I can't bear to be shouted at—you know that. I can feel a headache coming on."

Lord Brandford strove to control his voice. "Emma Armstead is gauche."

"Nonsense. She is well-bred and cultured, a credit to her school and to her sex."

"And she just happened to come hurtling down the bannisters. She just happened to knock your daughter flat and to cause her to sprain her ankle."

"Marcella has forgiven her. So have I."

"She'll encourage Marcella to slide down the bannisters."

"Rubbish. Anyway, ours aren't suitable for—" Lady Brandford stopped short before she confessed to her son her own sins in that direction.

Lord Brandford was too furious to notice. "Emma Armstead is wild and untamed."

"Poor motherless dear. Her mother died when she was five, you know, and her father, when she was not yet seventeen. She has no relations, no one in all the world. What she needs is a family. . .and a little affection."

"Bah!" The earl's face was the same sullen shade of red as his coat. "An abandoned squirrel or a stray kitten might respond to—"

"I like her. Why shouldn't I invite her?"

"Have you heard the stories circulating about her?"

"Stories? What stories?"

"It seems that upon one occasion, Miss Armstead organized a school-wide treasure hunt for pearls. The result was that Miss Foxall and Miss Quince had to spend the better part of the Easter holidays returning various sets of pearls to their rightful owners."

Lady Brandford eyed him judiciously. "You were not above getting into scrapes yourself when you were younger, Charles, you know." She reclined against the pink velvet cushions. "I could tell a few tales..."

Lord Brandford tapped his now-skateless foot menacingly on the flagstones of the hearth.

Lady Brandford's shoulders lifted slightly. "I am going to launch Emma Armstead into Society—and I am going to enjoy it!"

The earl snorted.

"Charles, Emma Armstead is a warmhearted, generous young lady. She wants to make friends, and—"

"She will not achieve it by hanging from the chandeliers."

"I beg your pardon?"

"Apparently, your protegée, Miss Emma Armstead, has a habit of swinging from the chandeliers in this Academy."

"Good gracious!" exclaimed his mother. Her lashes fluttered apprehensively. "I do hope she won't do that at our house in London. I'm sure they won't take the weight."

A faint smile curved the earl's lips. He rested his arm upon the mantelshelf. His fawn breeches contrasted well with the creamy marble.

"Mother dear—" he pressed his advantage "—you must see that it is impossible to launch Miss Armstead into Society."

Lady Brandford grimaced.

"We cannot invite her to Brandford House," he continued. "We cannot have her swinging from the chandeliers, sliding down the bannisters, organizing treasure hunts and generally causing havoc among our friends."

Lady Brandford looked helplessly at her son, and seemed to want to speak. Then she changed her mind and glanced past him into the leaping flames.

Lord Brandford knew he had won.

"Will you tell her?" he demanded. "Or shall I?"

His words were halfdrowned by the grandfather clock in the spacious entrance hall chiming the hour. It had not finished, when the doors of the drawing room were flung wide and Miss Quince came in, wearing a dress flowered like a meadow and her broadest smile. Following her was one of the younger girls, carrying a tea tray.

"I thought we might have tea in the drawing room," stated Miss Quince, "rather than in the dining hall."

"Oh, yes!" Lady Brandford was delighted. "That would be wonderful. Much better to have it here in private."

"Especially," murmured the earl, "as we have so many things to discuss."

Miss Quince's eyes flickered in alarm.

Miss Foxall, coming in directly after her, addressed their pupil. "Yes, you may leave that, Decima. We shall serve ourselves."

Decima, of the mouse-brown plaits, scurried away.

Miss Quince took refuge in arranging the tea things.

As the tea was passed, Miss Foxall turned to her guests. "What was it you wished to discuss?"

Lady Brandford dabbed a lump of butter onto a Wiltshire bun. These were a speciality of Houghton Regina and liberally flavoured with nutmeg. "My son has heard some curious stories about Miss Armstead."

"Such as?"

"Such as," supplied Lord Brandford, "that she was involved in an incident concerning a search for pearls..."

"Ah, yes, I do remember!" Miss Foxall smiled fondly at the recollection. "One of the teachers—to spare her blushes, I shall *not* name her—had a pearl necklace which, um, disappeared. Miss Armstead had only just arrived here. In fact, she came the day after the tragedy."

"Tragedy?" questioned Lady Brandford.

"Oh, it was a tragedy. Definitely!" declared Miss Quince.

"The pearl necklace," explained Miss Foxall, "was all that teacher possessed. She had intended to use it to provide herself with a pension in her old age."

"Whenever she could, she added a pearl to it," commented Miss Quince. "The pearls were all of the same size and colour—really quite lovely. And each year, the necklace grew."

"When Emma discovered these facts," continued Miss Foxall, "she realized how much the loss of the necklace would mean. She, therefore, conducted a search for it. It was found and returned to its ever-grateful owner."

"And that was the end of the matter." Miss Quince filled the teapot with hot water.

Lord Brandford frowned. "I, er, understood that you both spent the entire Easter holidays restoring various sets of pearls to their rightful owners..." He left his sentence unfinished.

Miss Foxall allowed herself an amused chuckle. "Some of the girls were a *little* overenthusiastic. Some, indeed, had no idea what a pearl looked like!"

Miss Quince laughed at the memory. "They brought us wooden beads painted white and milky glass ones!"

"However," concluded Miss Foxall, "we managed to give those necklaces back to their true owners, who were very understanding."

"Oh. I see." Lord Brandford was abashed. "How did the, er, teacher come to, uh, lose her pearls?"

"They were not lost," said Miss Quince. "They were stolen. That is what made it so dreadful. Had they been merely lost, they would naturally have turned up."

"Eventually," interposed Miss Foxall.

"But the teacher's jewel box had been rifled." Miss Quince made a gesture of disapprobation. "It was most unpleasant."

"And the thief?" asked Lord Brandford.

In accordance with the law, the thief ought to have been hanged.

"The thief was never caught," stated Miss Quince. "Another bun, Lady Brandford?"

"No, thank you."

"You have no idea who stole the pearls?" demanded the earl.

Miss Quince shook her head. "We never did find out. More tea?"

Both the earl and his mother accepted.

"Perhaps it is just as well," said Miss Foxall. "The thief was probably very young and may have learned to mend his—or her—ways since."

Miss Quince rang for more hot water.

"How completely different," exclaimed Lady Brandford when the fresh hot water had been brought, "it seems now that you have explained it!" She shot a triumphant glance at her son.

The earl's gaze dropped. His black lashes brushed his bronzed cheeks.

"I daresay the girls have, um, embellished the tale," conceded Miss Foxall. "I have noticed that certain stories tend to be embroidered, and can, on occasion, alter dramatically in the retelling."

"Exactly," murmured Miss Quince.

After handing her guests another cup of tea and refilling Miss Foxall's cup, Miss Quince poured herself some more tea.

"One may assume," remarked Lord Brandford dryly, "that Miss Armstead does not swing on the chandeliers?"

Miss Quince choked upon her tea.

Miss Foxall, however, met the earl's forthright gaze. "The late Colonel Armstead was a plain, blunt man. When his wife died, Miss Armstead was only five. He was left to bring up his daughter as he saw fit—"

"Entirely without the benefit of any female assistance," added Miss Quince.

Lady Brandford clicked her tongue. "Tsk. Tsk."

Miss Quince cut the seed cake and passed the slices round.

"The result was that—" Miss Foxall neatly separated a morsel of cake for herself with her cake fork "—when Miss Armstead was twelve, she was a trifle, um, unruly. But she is now nineteen, I am sure I need not remind you. In the intervening years, there have been vast improvements."

"But you have not yet succeeded in curbing certain unladylike propensities," persisted the earl.

"Miss Armstead swung on a chandelier once—seven years ago," allowed Miss Foxall reprovingly.

"Hrumph!"

"Are you referring to the incident with the bannisters?" enquired Miss Quince. "Because if you are, I assure you it will not happen again."

"I am referring to Miss Armstead's character."

"She is a trifle unconventional, certainly."

"Your restraint, Miss Quince, is admirable!"

"Lord Brandford," queried Miss Foxall, "may one ask where this is leading?"

Lady Brandford turned pink. "My son feels—" she fidgeted nervously "—that we ought to reconsider our invitation to Miss Armstead."

"Indeed!" Miss Foxall, in her striped raven-and-canary dress, resembled nothing so much as a tigress poised on the point of springing. "May one know the reason?"

"I consider it ill-advised," answered the Earl of Brandford haughtily, "for her to be in our house."

"Why?" demanded Miss Foxall coldly. "Do you intend to make improper advances to her?"

Lord Brandford was visibly shaken. "Certainly not!"

"Because if you do," added Miss Quince evenly, "we would naturally refuse to allow Miss Armstead to go with you. We must protect our charges at all times, you understand."

"Precisely," agreed Miss Foxall.

Lady Brandford, pale under her rouge, murmured, "You need have no fears on that respect. M-my son was merely...worried...in case it should be...too much for me. We—we shall of course be happy to have Emma." She had by then recovered and as she tossed her head, her manner was so reminiscent of her daughter that, but for the greying of her temples, they might have been twins. "Won't we, Charles?"

Lord Brandford's handsome face was set. "As you say, Mother dear."

As soon as they arrived in London, Lady Brandford sent to the kitchen to advise Cook to prepare a menu for a supper ball for five hundred people.

Once that matter was settled, Lady Brandford threw herself energetically into organizing Emma's coming-out ball.

Lady Brandford both knew and invited most of London Society. When the appointed evening arrived, Brandford House was full to bursting. Emma was presented to everyone who was anyone, from the Prince Regent downwards.

It was a taxing ordeal. Fortunately, however, Emma had been advised upon the subject by her dear departed father, Colonel Armstead.

"Coming-out balls," he had remarked, "are like inspection parades. So when your turn comes, see to it that your uniform is trim, your boots are polished and your helmet is on straight. Salute everyone with due deference, and you can't go wrong!"

Better even than this, Emma had been prepared for the great event by Miss Foxall and Miss Quince. With their help, Emma managed to smile her way through. And as soon as she had a spare minute, she wrote to thank them for their invaluable assistance.

"Never," she declared in her letter, "have I been introduced to so many complete strangers! There were battalions of them, no, squadrons, brigades, regiments, whole armies! If it had not been for the training you have given me, I should never have survived!"

THE NEXT BALL WAS EASIER, and the third one easier still. By the fifth, the other guests had stopped being a blur of names and faces. Emma was starting to make friends and to enjoy herself.

On this occasion, while Emma was talking to Lady Brandford's sister, a voice sounded in her ear. "This is my dance, I believe."

Emma turned her head to find that the Earl of Brandford stood beside her. She consulted her card.

"So it is!" A charming smile played about her soft coral lips. "I hope you will excuse me," she said to his aunt.

Lord Brandford offered her his arm and led her onto the dance floor.

The orchestra was playing a waltz. Emma's ivory silk gown, with its border of pink roses, swirled bewitchingly as she followed the Earl's lead.

Presently he observed, "You have been seeing a great deal of Lord Druce."

"John has been very kind to me since I first came to London."

"John?"

"We are on first-name terms now. Your mother insisted upon it."

His brown eyes flashed. "You must drop the acquaintance."

Emma stared at him. "Why?"

"You are monopolizing him. People will start to talk."

"Talk?" Emma frowned. "About what?"

Lord Brandford's lips compressed with momentary vexation. "When a man and a woman are constantly in each other's company to the exclusion of anyone else, people consider that they are a couple. This is what is happening with you and Lord Druce. If it continues, he may even be forced to...to propose to you."

"Umm," Emma glanced across the ballroom at Lord Druce.

He was on the edge of the polished dance floor. His hair gleamed in the candlelight and his pale blue coat blended in with the azure satin draperies. There was a small knot of people with him, who seemed to be laughing at some witticism.

"Oh, I think not," she answered Lord Brandford airily. "John does not favour me."

Emma expected the earl to object, but he did not. Instead, his arm tightened suddenly around Emma's slender waist. She uttered a gasp of astonishment, then a murmur of pleasure. *What a delicious feeling!* she reflected.

Lord Brandford's arm went tighter still.

Strange sensations, which were not at all unpleasant, shot through Emma. She revelled in his touch, and glanced up at him, dewy-eyed.

Lord Brandford's smouldering gaze, however, was not on his dancing partner. His burning eyes were fixed in the distance, on the other side of the ballroom, on a shimmering figure in silver tissue.

Emma's tiny bubble of happiness burst. "Who is she?"

She had not realized she had said the words aloud, until he replied. "Miss Lavinia Smythe. Allow me to introduce you."

Emma had no chance to protest. The waltz was over and Lord Brandford led her straight to where Lord Druce's party were amusing themselves.

The introductions were quickly made. As soon as they were over, Miss Lavinia Smythe pouted provocatively at the earl, and said, "Charles! We have not danced once this evening. Will you not dance with me?"

"I should be delighted." Lord Brandford offered her his arm.

Emma watched them as they took their places for a cotillion.

Charles really is the finest-looking gentleman in the whole of London! she thought. At least he would be, if only he wouldn't scowl so!

It had not been apparent to Emma, when she had first met him, how sensitive his features were. Of course, she mused, it hadn't really helped that he was absolutely livid at the time. In fact, he had been furious with her from the instant she had collided with Lady Marcella, had glowered at her the entire time they were at the Houghton Academy for Young Ladies, and had lowered at her like an imminent thunderstorm, all the way from Houghton Regina to London.

Then, his brow had seemed settled in a permanent frown. It had been ages before Emma had discovered what a charming smile he had. Emma remembered the incident clearly. She conjured it up, allowing it to blot out the realities of the ballroom.

IT HAD HAPPENED SUDDENLY and unexpectedly.

One morning, a couple of weeks before, Lady Brandford had decided to go shopping with Lady Marcella and Emma. Lord Brandford had elected to join them.

At one point, the earl went to Protices for a hat, while the ladies went into Messrs. William Labbett & Sons for dress material.

Emma had selected the fabrics she wanted, but Lady Brandford and Lady Marcella had not, and they were not disposed to hurry.

Eventually, when they took such an unconscionably long time to admire the various silks and muslins on offer, Emma became restless and returned to the carriage, which was parked in Glasshouse Street, on the edge of Soho.

Lord Brandford had been nowhere in sight.

While Emma sat in the carriage, making a note of her purchases, the bell of the muffin man clanged in the distance. Nearer and nearer it came, and with it, his harsh croaking chant.

> My bell I'm a-ringing
> And merrily singing
> Muffins. Fresh muffins.
> All hot on my tray.

Emma turned her head as the muffin man walked by, and she noticed a group of children watching him. They ranged from three to nine years old. They had bare feet and hungry eyes. They said nothing, but the wistfulness in their gaze spoke for them.

Emma could not resist their silent appeal. She put away her notebook, rolled down the carriage window and beckoned to the muffin man.

"Yes, my lady." He was a Cockney—respectful, but not subservient. "What is your ladyship's pleasure?"

Emma smiled. It was the carriage, of course: anyone riding in an equipage as grand as this, must be "my lady," and even if she weren't, a little flattery never hurt with a paying customer.

"Do you see those children over there?"

"Yes," answered the muffin man, as bright and chirpy as a sparrow. "Greedy little beggars, ain't they?"

"Give them each a muffin and I'll pay for it."

"Ne-ver! Oooh, you are generous, my lady! Did you 'ear that, you little beggars? You're to 'ave a muffin each!"

They had heard. Their eyes had lit up and eagerly they had come forward with their hands outstretched.

It was as Emma had finished paying the muffin man—at the very moment he had touched his hat to her—that Lord Brandford had appeared.

He had glanced at the children, eyes shiny, mouths stuffed with muffins, and all at once a brilliant smile had illuminated his features.

It had made Emma's heart turn over.

SLOWLY, THE VISION FADED. The music, the people, the warmth of the ballroom reasserted themselves.

Emma continued to study Lord Brandford. His attire was, as ever, perfect: jet-black coat, white knee breeches, white stockings, silver-buckled shoes and kid gloves.

He seems to have been poured into his clothes! she mused. He made every other man look as if their clothes were borrowed from their big brothers!

Frederick Nunney broke the silence. "She is lovely!"

Emma followed the direction of his gaze. "Yes," she agreed.

Lavinia Smythe was, like Emma, a blue-eyed blonde. Though she was only a year older than Emma, she had been "out" for four Seasons.

"She floats as she dances," commented Emma.

"Lavinia?"

"Yes."

"How poetic! She is a graceful dancer, certainly." Frederick Nunney took a pinch of snuff. "She'll make an excellent Lady Brandford!"

Emma's heart plummeted. "They—they are engaged?"

Frederick Nunney laughed. "No. But everyone expects it. Brandford has warned us off."

"Warned *you* off, you mean," interrupted Lord Druce. "He has said nothing to me. Besides, I—" He checked himself abruptly, then went on lamely, "Lavinia and I are old friends."

"Just you try and make a play for her! Brandford roused—"

"The devil with Brandford!"

"For heaven's sake, don't let there be any quarrelling!" urged Fanny Peplow.

"Fanny, you are too anxious," Lord Druce answered his cousin. "Freddy was only teasing me, as usual. Of course, I know Brandford means to marry Lavinia. It is common knowledge. But she hasn't accepted him—"

"Yet," completed Frederick Nunney.

Emma bit her lip.

If that is so, she told herself, *I must definitely not allow myself to fall in love with Charles.*

And how, asked her heart, *are you going to stop yourself?*

I shall be firm, decided Emma silently. *Very firm.*

Bah! countered her heart. *It's too late. Much too late, you dreamer! You fell head over heels in love with Charles weeks ago. You just never troubled to admit it to yourself... before now.*

CHAPTER FOUR

"MAY I HAVE THIS DANCE?" requested Lord Druce.

"Of course." Emma flashed a brilliant smile as she accepted. Once more she whirled around the ballroom. Lord Druce was a good dancer and a pleasant companion. She was sorry when the music stopped and the dance was over.

Lord Druce had scarcely taken her to the edge of the floor, when Emma felt a pair of fingers on her elbow. She turned round to find the Earl of Brandford at her side, his eyes flaming angrily. Without speaking, he fairly dragged her into the library.

"I believe I told you," said Lord Brandford evenly as he locked the door behind him, "that you were to cease your acquaintance with Lord Druce."

Emma pouted. "John asked me to dance. As this is a ball, I could hardly refuse."

The earl gritted his teeth. "Nevertheless, you will refuse him next time he asks."

"I shall not."

"What did you say?"

"I said *'I shall not.'*"

Lord Brandford took a deep breath to steady himself. "When you came here, it was on the understanding that you would behave yourself with propriety—"

"And so I have! I have been very good." Emma's rose-painted fan waved tantalizingly back and forth. "As you know perfectly well, I have been nice to everyone. I shall continue to be nice . . . to *everyone*. If John wishes to dance with me, then he may dance with me."

"You little fool!"

"I am neither little nor a fool."

"Do you know what is going to happen if you dance with him again?"

"Nothing will happen."

"This will happen."

Lord Brandford seized her in his arms and pressed his lips against hers.

Emma's first thought was to struggle.

Her next thought was, *Well, perhaps I should find out what it is like being kissed by Charles.*

The thought after that was, *Mmm! I rather like Charles's kisses!*

As she made no resistance, Lord Brandford kept on kissing her. His arms wound more tightly around her, and his lips sought hers with an insistence which would not be denied.

A sharp knocking at the door broke them apart.

"Emma? Charles? Are you in there?" It was Lady Brandford.

Abruptly the earl's arms fell to his sides.

Emma looked at him. His eyes were shocked and bewildered, as if she had initiated those kisses—not he.

"Your mouth has carmine on it, Charles," she murmured.

He drew forth a white cambric handkerchief and savagely removed the smudge.

"This door is locked!" muttered Lady Brandford.

Swiftly the earl moved forward and unlocked it.

"Charles," began his mother, "what are you doing . . . ?"

"Lecturing me, Lady Brandford," answered Emma brightly.

"Lecturing Emma?" Lady Brandford questioned her son. "Why? What has she done?"

"She has been seeing too much of Lord Druce." Lord Brandford's voice was slightly unsteady. "People will talk."

Lady Brandford clicked her tongue. "You are making a mountain out of a molehill, Charles. Come with me, Emma, before people begin talking about you and my son!"

WHEN EMMA WAS SAFELY ensconced amidst a large crowd of ladies and gentlemen, Lady Brandford returned to the library.

"Charles? Charles? Where are you? I particularly want to talk to you, Charles!"

Lady Brandford frowned.

Where can he be? she wondered. It was imperative that she speak to him. That look on his face! The way he stared at Emma! *He is in love with her! I know he is!*

Such a shattering discovery had to be discussed, calmly, rationally—before her beloved son did something foolish. *Now where can he be?* she asked herself again.

Outside in the street, she heard horses' hooves. She went to the curtains and parted them. Down below, she saw Lord Brandford assisting Lavinia into her carriage. He followed her in, and the carriage sped away in the darkness.

"No!" Lady Brandford's lips compressed in a firm line. "Oh, Charles! Don't do it! Please don't propose to Lavinia!"

"MR. DE TROYES!" announced Wooster, the butler.

Lord Brandford rose to his feet. "Louis! Come in!"

"Charles!" Louis de Troyes shook his host warmly by the hand. "I did not expect you to be up and dressed at this hour!" he teased.

The Earl of Brandford's black eyebrows arched. "I am not *that* late a riser!"

"But you were dancing all last night, into the small hours of this morning, and with such pretty young ladies. I quite envied you!"

The Earl of Brandford shrugged. "Most of them were tiresome flibbertigibbets."

"Ah! The exceptions being your mother, your sister and Lavinia Smythe. Yes?"

"Yes." Perhaps it was because Louis de Troyes had not mentioned her name that suddenly an image of Emma rose in the Earl's mind. It had a disturbing effect on him. He could not meet his friend's gaze. "What brings you here this afternoon? It was not to see me, surely?"

"I had an urgent communication from Lady Brandford."

"From my mother? What about?"

Louis de Troyes lifted his shoulders expressively. "I do not know. But she was most insistent that I come at once."

The words were scarcely out of his mouth when the study door was flung wide and Lady Brandford glided in.

A liveried footman closed the door behind her.

"Louis! I am so glad you have come! Charles dear, would you do me a small favour?"

"Certainly."

"Would you take this to the post office for me? Immediately?"

Lord Brandford sighed wearily. "I shall send one of the footmen—" His hand moved towards the plush bellrope.

"No. No." His mother prevented him. "You must go yourself. It is very important, and I don't want to trust it to a servant. Please, Charles?" She besought him beguilingly.

Lord Brandford grimaced. He put the letter into his breast pocket, bowed and excused himself.

As soon as he had gone, Lady Brandford draped herself across one of the burgundy velvet chairs. "Louis, something dreadful has happened!"

"Madam, I am all attention."

"You must help!"

"Anything that I can do," he assured her. "Is it ... Marcella?"

"No, worse than that. It is Charles."

"Charles?"

"He has fallen in love."

"But that is wonderful! I am very happy for him." Then, seeing her face, "Aren't you?"

"Yes. Yes." She wrung her hands. "Unfortunately he doesn't know it, and he is going to marry the wrong woman."

Louis de Troyes sat down smartly opposite his hostess. "That is indeed very grave. But surely Charles ... I mean ... he is older than I am. He is twenty-seven. He can manage—"

"Manage? Nonsense! He is as obstinate and as pig-headed as his father. He'll never admit it. Just as Henry never admitted he was in love with me—until I dragged it out of him."

Louis de Troyes eyed her curiously. "Do you mean ... yours was a love match?"

"Certainly!"

"Your pardon ... I—"

"I know," interrupted Lady Brandford impatiently. "Everyone was convinced it was a marriage of convenience. Henry was so much older than I—" a sigh of longing escaped her "—I couldn't have married him had I not loved him. And when he died ..." A handkerchief appeared, and two tears were hastily wiped away. "I cannot let Charles marry without love, for it would destroy him." Her voice lowered almost to a whisper. "It would kill me."

"I understand, but—"

"Do you see? Then you must act—now. Beat Charles into submission if necessary...."

Louis de Troyes laughed softly. "Come, come, Lady Brandford! I cannot beat Charles into submission! He is my friend!"

"I didn't mean it literally!"

Louis de Troyes gestured helplessly. "I don't see how I can help! I do not move in the same circles as Charles...and you know what he can be like."

"But you are a man—"

"A stranger."

"Practically one of the family! You can think of something. You will know how to deal with Charles where I would not. If his father were alive, it would be another matter!" Tears threatened to flow once more. "Alas! My poor darling Henry has been dead these two—no, it is nearly three—years now! I appeal to you, Louis! You cannot refuse!"

"Naturally, as I have said, I will do anything I can to help. It is just that—" he spread his hands wide "—I don't think there is anything that I can do. If I were to meddle, I might simply make matters worse."

Lady Brandford sniffed.

"Who is the young lady?"

"Didn't I say? I thought you knew. I thought you guessed. It's Emma."

"Emma?" He gaped at her.

"Yes, Emma. Charles is in love with Emma. I saw it in his eyes last night." Lady Brandford twisted her handkerchief this way and that. "It was a revelation. I never suspected it. I don't know how I could have been so blind!"

Louis de Troyes coughed. "Forgive me, but...they seem to be always fighting, snapping at each other."

"Pshaw! It means nothing. Henry was exactly the same. Charles is a rough wooer. Fine verses, pretty words...a formal proposal on bended knee...a woman has to look elsewhere for those."

Louis de Troyes was still dazed. "But are you sure he is in love? With Emma? People say... people say he detests her."

"Fiddle-faddle. Of course Charles is in love with Emma. He is head over ears in love with Emma."

"In that case, why worry? He will marry her, won't he?"

Lady Brandford was shaking her head. "He is going ahead with this ridiculous plan to marry Lavinia. He proposed to her last night, and she accepted—the goose!"

Louis de Troyes remained tactfully silent.

"He has given her a ring," continued Lady Brandford. "She has set the date."

"When is it?"

"May! Less than five months! It must be stopped. The engagement must be broken. For Charles's sake!"

"Lady Brandford, haven't you forgotten Lavinia? She is bound to be hurt, if—"

"Hurt? Lavinia? Hah!"

"Lady Brandford..."

"Lavinia Smythe doesn't love Charles. She loves his title and she loves my jewels. Oh, she *likes* Charles well enough. She will probably be quite *kind* to him if she becomes his wife."

"Are you saying she has, er, inveigled Charles into marriage?"

Lady Brandford shrugged. "It is possible. I don't know how cunning she is. But she does not love him, that I am certain of. And I swear she will not have a single piece of my jewellery. Not so much as a crushed-glass bauble." Lady Brandford rose and walked across the room to the French windows. "How cold it is outside. And how foggy! I do hope Charles is wrapped up warmly. I don't want him to catch cold."

"ISN'T THAT CHARLES going past?" asked Lady Marcella. Emma pressed her nose against the window of the upstairs drawing room. "Yes. He has just taken a letter out of his breast pocket. He is looking at it. Now he has put it back again. He is walking on."

"Tsk. It must be that awful thing Mother dear was writing. Some business involving Father dear's estate. I wonder why Charles is taking it? Oh, I know. It is to be paid for in advance. Why are you sitting on the windowsill, Emma?"

"Because there isn't a window seat."

"But why sit so close the window?"

"So I can see better. The light is very bad, especially with this mist coming down. I don't want to light a candle and—"

A gust of cold air made them turn around.

A maid stood half in the room, half in the chilly corridor.

"Miss Lavinia Smythe!" she announced.

"Lavinia! Do come in!" Lady Marcella advanced to meet her.

"Marcella!" Lavinia embraced her. "I can't tell you how pleased I was to see you at the ball last night. I am so glad your ankle is better."

"Oh, it is quite healed." Lady Marcella smiled welcomingly. "Have you met our guest, Miss Armstead?"

"Yes. We were introduced last night." She inclined her head in Emma's direction. "It was decided that we should all be on Christian name terms."

Emma returned the acknowledgement. "So much less stuffy," she added.

"Hmm." Lavinia wrinkled her dainty little nose.

"Is something the matter?" enquired Lady Marcella.

"I—I am not sure...." Lavinia Smythe uttered an embarrassed laugh. "There is a strange...odour."

"Oh. It's probably because the room has not been aired since we got home last night," answered Lady Marcella.

"I'll open the window." She glanced from one to the other of her guests. Lavinia was wearing a white fur-lined pelisse over her milky sarcenet gown. Emma had on only a lime-green woollen dress. "You don't mind, do you, Emma?"

"No, of course not."

Emma leaned back to allow Lady Marcella to push the sash window up.

"Oh, thanks awfully!" Lavinia inhaled deeply. "Ah! That is better. I do like a breath of fresh air!"

Lady Marcella and Emma exchanged glances.

"I wouldn't call it fresh," countered Emma. "Not in this mist."

Lavinia shrugged deprecatingly. Then suddenly she smiled. "Marcella, I had to come. I wanted to tell you the good news myself."

"What good news?" questioned Lady Marcella.

"We are to become sisters!" Lavinia withdrew her white kid glove and revealed a cluster of sparkling diamonds upon her finger. "Charles has proposed at last!"

"Oh!" gasped Lady Marcella. "Congratulations!"

Emma's response was rather different. *I have lost him!* she thought poignantly.

Her body jerked in agony. She half rose from her place. She lost her balance. She slipped from the windowledge and fell out of the window.

Lady Marcella screamed as Emma disappeared from view. Lavinia Smythe's reaction was far more ladylike: she fainted.

CHAPTER FIVE

EMMA WAS SUSPENDED HALFWAY between heaven and earth. Her eyes were shut tight.

I can't look! she thought.

Curiosity compelled her to open her eyes, however. She was staring down at the tips of some viciously spiked railings, which were pointing directly at her white breasts. Emma swallowed. She felt a sharp pain along her left leg, and guessed that it was caught in the sash cord.

That must be what is still holding me up, she reflected.

"Marcella!" she called weakly. "Help me!"

Lady Marcella leaned out of the window. She grabbed hold of Emma's left leg. "I've got you. I'm hanging on to you."

"Pull me up!"

"I can't!"

"Ask Lavinia to help you."

"She has fainted."

Emma gulped. The spiked railings leered menacingly at her. She realized if she fell onto them, it would be an agonizing death.

"What are we going to do?"

"I don't know," responded Lady Marcella.

It was then Emma perceived that she still held her book in her hand. She glanced around. The study was illuminated and she could see Lady Brandford within.

Emma extended her book as far as it would go. She tapped upon the French windows.

"What is that peculiar noise?" demanded Lady Brandford.

The tapping came again.

Lady Brandford looked out. Her eyes widened. She stifled a horrified shriek.

Louis de Troyes was on his feet. He rushed to the French windows and opened them wide. "Emma! What is going on?"

"I slipped!" wailed Emma. "Please help me!"

⁓ The French windows gave upon a mock balcony, fenced off by a black-painted metal guardrail. It was but a foot wide.

Louis de Troyes balanced himself upon it and carefully stretched his arms upwards. He had to clasp Emma in a rather indelicate manner.

"Please forgive me," he murmured.

"I'll forgive you anything, Louis!" Emma vowed. "Anything! Only please don't let me fall onto those railings!"

"Courage! It will not come to that." Louis de Troyes frowned. "What is keeping your leg up there?"

"The sash cord. It is caught around my ankle."

"Who is in the drawing room?"

"Marcella."

"Marcella!" called Louis de Troyes.

"Louis!" His beloved replied.

"Try to disentangle Emma's ankle from the sash cord. Then let her down gently."

"Yes."

"And Marcella..."

"Yes?"

"Please don't fall down yourself!"

"I won't. I'm hanging on to the window frame."

It seemed an eternity, though it was only a couple of seconds before Emma felt her foot freed. Her body descended with a sudden whoosh and she fell against Louis de Troyes' chest. She was in his arms.

Tenderly, solicitously, he brought her into the study.

Emma was shaking like a leaf. All at once, relief at being safe flooded through her.

"Oh, Louis! I don't know how to thank you!" Impulsively, she flung her arms about his neck and kissed him.

"May I ask what is going on?" Lord Brandford stood in the doorway, his brown eyes burning with anger, his mouth twisted into a supercilious sneer.

Louis de Troyes hastily stepped away from Emma. "Your pardon, I—"

Lady Brandford decided to change the subject. "Did you post my letter, Charles?"

"Yes," he answered curtly, then focused his attention upon the miscreants once more. "Well?"

"Louis saved my life," answered Emma softly. "I gave him a kiss because I was grateful, very grateful."

"Louis saved your life?"

"I—I fell out of the window...."

"She made a complete spectacle of herself." Lavinia Smythe had recovered, and Lady Marcella had accompanied her downstairs. But whereas Lady Marcella had gone straight to Louis de Troyes's side, Lavinia remained framed in the entrance to the study. Her face was still pale, her nose in the air and her blue eyes fastened upon Lord Brandford. "She hung upside down. Her petticoat—her petticoat, Charles!—was not the only thing she exposed. The entire street could see. I was so mortified, Charles, that I fainted away!" Lavinia's ringed hand passed across her forehead.

Lord Brandford's accusing gaze travelled to Emma.

"I did not do it on purpose!" Emma asserted.

"No, of course you didn't, dear," soothed Lady Brandford. "Charles, the poor child has had a most dreadful shock. Don't you think—"

The Earl of Brandford was not listening. His eyes met Emma's. "May I ask how you came to do it?"

"Charles, really I—" began Lady Brandford. She saw where his gaze was directed. "Emma..."

Emma was not listening to her, either. Passionately, she interrupted, "Why can't you have decent window seats? Why can't you have proper sash cords?"

"I—I—" spluttered the earl.

"If you had had decent window seats and proper sash cords, this would never have happened!" She was close to tears as she rounded on Lavinia. "And the entire street could *not* see! The fog is so thick I doubt if *anyone* saw!"

"*I* saw!" declared Lavinia primly.

"Well, you needn't have looked!" retorted Emma.

"It was impossible not to look!"

"Hah! Don't blame me because your eyes see and your nose smells everything they shouldn't. If it hadn't been for you, the drawing room window would never have been opened. You and your fresh air!"

Lavinia was a picture of wounded indignation.

"How dare you speak to my fiancée in that way!" raged Lord Brandford.

"How dare *she* speak to *me* that way!" countered Emma. "How dare *you*! I think you are both perfectly beastly." Emma's voice quavered. "And I hope...you'll be...very happy...together." With that, she burst into tears and ran from the room.

"Now see what you've done!" exclaimed Lady Marcella.

The Earl of Brandford was mute and helpless.

"*I'll* look after Emma." Lady Brandford left the study in high dudgeon. "Marcella, Charles, please attend to our guests." She slammed the door behind her.

Lord Brandford took a step towards Lavinia. His lips parted as if he were about to speak.

"There is no need to trouble yourself," she said, forestalling him. She looked as if she had stepped into something rather distasteful. "I shall not be staying."

"But you have only just arrived, Lavinia," protested Lord Brandford. "Surely..."

"You must forgive me, Charles. I am not well. The unpleasantness which has occurred has grieved me most dreadfully. The way Emma spoke to me! I, who have never done anything to hurt her!"

"I am sure Emma did not mean it," Lady Marcella interjected. "She was extremely overwrought. Charles has that effect on her."

"Charles?" Lavinia blinked.

"Did you not notice how he snapped at her?"

"I did not snap!" said Lord Brandford crossly.

Lady Marcella ignored him. "They do not get on. In fact, Charles fought against us having her here." She glanced defiantly at her brother.

The Earl of Brandford glared at her.

"Oh, she is *your* friend!" observed Lavinia.

"Yes, indeed. We met at the Houghton Academy for Young Ladies. She was one of the pupils," explained Lady Marcella. "*I* liked her, and Mother dear was much taken with her. But Charles...!" She shrugged despairingly.

Lavinia's blue eyes flickered from Lady Marcella to Lord Brandford to Louis de Troyes.

"It is the truth," Louis de Troyes weighed in. "Charles never has a kind word to say for Emma—or *to* her."

"You exaggerate," muttered the earl between clenched teeth.

Louis's shoulders lifted meaningfully.

Lord Brandford's face turned several shades darker, and he tugged at his heavy linen cravat as if it choked him.

Lavinia advanced and laid her hand gently on his arm. "Darling Charles, don't be angry."

"How I can be anything but?"

"You might be kinder to Emma. It would prevent these little, er, mishaps, you know."

Lord Brandford's nostrils flared. "I don't see how."

"She might lose her...her nervousness. And then these...embarrassing incidents would cease."

Lord Brandford drummed his fingers exasperatedly on the top of a rosewood cabinet.

"Do try to be charitable to her, Charles," Lavinia besought him. "I am sure she would appreciate it. For she is— so I have been told—all alone in the world."

"IS SOMETHING THE MATTER, Lady Brandford?" enquired Emma, concerned.

Lady Brandford was stretched upon the sofa, with her eyes closed. "Yes. I have a perfectly frightful headache."

"Can I get you something?"

"No, thank you. Only tell me when the banging has stopped."

"Banging?"

"Can you not hear it? It has been reverberating through the house since breakfast time. And now it is echoing and reechoing through my poor throbbing head!"

"I have been out all morning with Marcella. We have been driving in Hyde Park. Marcella said it was the done thing. We met a great number of gentlemen." Emma dimpled. "But if the truth be known, I think Marcella went there to see Louis."

Lady Brandford laughed softly. "Ah, yes. Charles is going to have to give in on that...eventually." She fetched a deep sigh. "But did you hear nothing when you came in?"

"No. Why? What is happening?"

"Charles, for some reason, has decided to have the front windows furnished with window seats. And he is so like his father—he will *not* wait!"

Emma stared at her.

Is it? she wondered. It couldn't be on account of what she had said, could it? *No, of course not,* she answered herself silently. *Charles wouldn't do that for me. He hates me. He is going to marry Lavinia—the wretch!*

Her heart ached. She hardly heard Lady Brandford murmuring, "Good gracious! No wonder you couldn't hear it. It has stopped! How peculiar. I could have sworn..."

He hates me, Emma kept thinking, *but I love him. I love him! I love him! I love him!* her heart chanted.

And he was engaged to Lavinia: suitable, graceful, perfect, proper Lavinia.

"AND I ACCEPTED," Lady Brandford was saying.

"You *what*!" exploded her son.

Lady Brandford was affronted. "There is no need to shout, Charles. I am not deaf."

"What is the matter?" demanded Lady Marcella, coming into the study, with Emma and Louis in tow.

"Nothing," returned Lord Brandford coolly.

"Merely," explained his mother, much to his chagrin, "that Lavinia has been invited to a masquerade at Lord Druce's. She would very much like to go, she said, but she wanted my advice. I thought she should go. And, on perusing our invitations, I saw we had been invited, as well. So I accepted."

"We?" queried Lady Marcella. "All of us?"

"Yes, Emma and Louis, too," replied Lady Brandford. "I don't see how you can object to that, Charles."

Lord Brandford turned away from the group ranged about the study. He walked to the window and stared at the Portland stone houses across the street; lost in thought, he gnawed his lower lip. "You should have consulted me first, Mother dear."

"Tsk! Charles, really!" scolded Lady Brandford. "You are obsessed with John."

"You exaggerate!" countered the earl. "I merely feel that it would have been better to have refused his invitation."

His mother sighed exasperatedly. "You used not to have anything against him."

"I still have nothing against him," her son assured her. "However, I have observed that Emma is seeing too much of him. If she continues to be forever in his company..."

"Which she isn't," Lady Marcella interjected.

Lord Brandford glowered at her. "People will talk," he finished frostily.

"Rubbish!" retorted Lady Brandford. "Anyway, I think it is very handsome of John to include all of us, and I told him so when I accepted on *everyone's* behalf."

Lord Brandford's lips curled into a snarl.

"If you don't wish to attend," said Emma helpfully, "you don't have to."

Lord Brandford ground his teeth. "It is *you* who ought not to go—not *me*."

"But I like John, and this masquerade sounds rather fun."

"It is not fun. It is a menace. The more you see of Lord Druce, the greater the danger to your reputation!"

Emma shook her head. "No. You are quite wrong," she stated sweetly. "I am sure John will see to it that my reputation does not suffer."

"You seem to place great faith in him."

"I trust him, certainly. He is so kind, so considerate." And then, feeling the earl had been unfair to Lord Druce, she added, "Such a *gentleman*."

Flames shot out of Lord Brandford's eyes. "What do you mean?"

"Why, just that if there is any question of propriety," replied Emma, "John will, um, do the right thing."

"Yes, of course he will," agreed Lady Brandford blithely. "So you see, there is absolutely nothing to make a fuss about."

"LADY BRANDFORD! Welcome to The Rookery!" Lord Druce was dressed in the costume of an Elizabethan courtier. He doffed his high-crowned hat with a flourish.

Lady Brandford inclined her head in acknowledgement. Her magnificent emerald-green turban shimmered in the candlelight.

"I am so glad you could *all* come," said Lord Druce with careful emphasis, bowing.

Emma noticed that the cartwheel ruff about his neck and the short chocolate cloak that hung from his shoulders gave him an air of roguishness which suited him.

"How are you, Charles?" continued Lord Druce.

"Very well. You must congratulate me, for I am now engaged to this charming young lady," Lord Brandford replied, bringing Lavinia forward.

A shadow crossed Lord Druce's countenance. "So I have heard, and I am very happy for you both. When is the wedding to be?"

"In May," responded Lavinia.

For a second, it seemed to Emma as if Lord Druce had issued a challenge and Lavinia Smythe had picked up the gauntlet he had flung down and thrown it back at him. Then Emma shook her head as if to clear it, telling herself she must be mistaken.

"We thought it would be the best time," added Lavinia, "when the flowers are at their prettiest."

"Yes, of course." Lord Druce sounded strained. "Marcella, you must let me have the next dance with you. Your Mary Queen of Scots dress perfectly complements my costume. Come, let us be off!"

Lady Marcella, laughing, went with him.

Emma noticed that Lavinia grimaced, but again told herself she must be imagining it.

"Come, Lavinia! This dance is mine," declared Lord Brandford.

As he led her to the centre of the dance floor, Louis de Troyes turned to Lady Brandford, saying, "May I?" He offered her his arm.

"Oh, no, no. I chose this costume expressly so that I would not be asked to dance," replied her ladyship. "You cannot be so cruel as to compel me!"

"Not dance? But you love dancing!"

"Tonight I do not love dancing. I wish to stand on the sidelines and observe. Dance with Emma, Louis. I insist upon it."

CHAPTER SIX

"WHAT AN ODD COUPLE WE MAKE!" Emma declared as the dance began.

Louis de Troyes had chosen a French costume from the reign of Louis XIV. A large black wig hid his fair hair, and a mass of ruffles fell over his hands. Emma was an Arcadian shepherdess, adorned with garlands of flowers.

"No more so than Charles and Lavinia."

Emma glanced at them.

Lavinia had come as Helen of Troy. A golden diadem graced her head. Her hair was swept up in the Greek manner, with a cascade of ringlets falling down her neck.

Lord Brandford was a Cavalier with a sky-blue silk doublet and breeches of the same fabric.

"Hmm." Emma remarked on how little pleased Lord Brandford and Lavinia Smythe seemed to be in each other's company. *Perhaps they aren't in love,* she mused, and hope surged within her. "I see what you mean," she responded.

When the dance was over, Emma was claimed by another gentleman—and another, and another. She lost touch with her own party and it was a couple of hours later when Lord Druce came to her side.

"Emma! At last!" He kissed her hand. "May I have this dance?"

Emma smiled. "I am rather tired. I would prefer to rest."

He put his head to one side. "Are you avoiding me?"

Emma stared at him. "Of course not!"

"You certainly seem to have been avoiding me of late."

"I have not!"

"Yet when I call, you are always out."

"I—" She stopped abruptly. "Ah! I see what has happened. It is Charles's doing." And then, under her breath, she added, "The scurvy knave."

Surprise and consternation showed in Lord Druce's face. "What do you mean?"

"Charles says we are seeing too much of each other."

Lord Druce flinched. "I—I did not know he was still..."

"Still what?"

"We cannot talk here." He led her away from the crowds to one of the rooms not open to his guests.

It was an old-fashioned chamber, with a white moulded ceiling and linenfold panelling. As the fire was unlit, it was quite cool, and Emma needed a shawl.

"What is it?"

Lord Druce sighed. "How much do you know about Charles?"

"Very little, except that he has the devil's own temper and seems always to be cross with me." Emma arranged herself on an elaborately carved black oak seat. She looked enquiringly up at her host.

"Charles and I and the late Lord Brandford all held commissions in the army. We were commanded by Sir John Moore at that time. When Sir John died, Wellington—he was then Sir Arthur Wellesley—took over. At Talavera he won a great victory."

"Yes. My father died there."

"Ah! So you know something of the battle."

"You need not explain it to me."

"There were a good many casualties. One of them was Charles's father."

"I knew that."

"Do you know how he died?"

"No."

"A bullet ripped him apart. It was a nasty, gaping wound, and there was nothing the surgeons could do. He did not die immediately. He lived in pain for several hours, and finally died in Charles's arms, apologizing to everyone for upsetting them with his groans."

"How awful!" cried Emma. "Poor Charles! Poor Lady Brandford! Poor Marcella!"

"Yes. It was dreadful for the family. Charles was terribly shaken. He spoke hardly a word for weeks after. It was I who told the family."

Emma frowned.

"Charles was livid. He said I should have kept the details from them, but..."

"They asked you and you could not refuse?" guessed Emma.

He nodded. "If they had not heard it from me, they would have heard it from somebody else. These things cannot be kept hidden, and I was afraid they would be given a wildly exaggerated version."

"Yes, yes. I know what you mean. I heard from several people about m-my f-father."

"Charles was furious with me 'for interfering' as he called it. He told me to keep away from his family in future. He—he wasn't himself. His father meant a great deal to him." Lord Druce plucked at the slashed sleeves of his scarlet doublet.

"Charles left the army?"

"Yes. The late Lord Brandford wished it. As he was dying, he begged Charles to give up his commission and go back home. He told him to involve himself in other matters which would help the war effort, which Charles has done—very successfully."

"Ah." The sound was as noncommittal as Emma could make it.

"Charles before Talavera was a different Charles. He was more happy-go-lucky, merrier, more approachable. Since then, he has become distant and—"

"Cold?"

"No. Charles is not cold. But he has greater difficulty in showing his feelings. I thought when I returned on leave that he had at last got over his father's death, but now I see it is still eating into him."

"And you believe that is why he has behaved as he has done?"

"Yes."

Emma pursed her lips.

"You don't agree?"

Emma shook her head. "It doesn't make sense, John. I can accept that Charles would have been angry at the time. But to bear a grudge for nearly three years, and to involve me..."

Lord Druce paced up and down in front of her. "You think there is another reason he has, er, discouraged my visits?"

"There must be."

Her companion looked puzzled at first, then suddenly stricken. Guilt showed in his eyes.

Emma regarded him curiously.

His expression altered again, then he laughed softly. "I could be wrong, of course. No one would be happier than I if—if Charles has forgiven me."

There was a brief silence.

Emma broke it. "Shall we rejoin the others?"

Lord Druce smiled warmly. "Why not?" He held out his hand to Emma. "The supper rooms will be open now. Perhaps you would like some refreshments?"

"WHERE HAVE YOU BEEN?" demanded the Earl of Brandford.

Emma faced him boldly. "I have been dancing. It has been such fun. Where have *you* been?"

"I have been on the dance floor since we arrived. Strange that I did not see you!"

"Not really. There are a great many people here."

Lord Brandford fumed.

"Do you find it too warm?" enquired Emma. "You look rather flushed. Would you like a nice, cool drink? They are serving a delicious iced punch in the supper rooms."

"No, thank you." He paused, then repeated, "Where have you been?"

"But I told you, I—"

"'Have been dancing. It has been such fun,'" he mimicked.

Emma let him see that she had taken umbrage, but he was not disposed to placate her.

"And...?" he growled.

"And?" Emma's blue eyes were blank.

His mouth set in a grim line. "Where else have you been? And what else have you been doing?"

"You are not going to be disagreeable again, are you? Please, do not shout at me or bite my head off, Charles. I am enjoying myself. I am not going to allow you to spoil it for me." She made as if to go.

His hand tightened upon her wrist. "Who have you been with?"

"Tsk!" Emma clicked her tongue. "You may as well know. You'll find out anyway. I had supper with John, and before that, I had a long talk with him. He has been trying to see me, and—"

"*I* told him you were out, yes."

"You shouldn't have done that. It was impolite." Emma detached his hand from her wrist. "Miss Foxall and Miss Quince would not approve. They taught us that when someone calls and you are in, you should say that you are in. You should receive them.''

''Miss Foxall and Miss Quince have not met Lord Druce.''

Emma pouted. ''John said that you were cross with him because he told your mother and your sister how your father died.''

The moment she had uttered the words, Emma wished she had not.

Lord Brandford looked as if he had been split open with an axe. He closed his eyes. His face went pale. For an awful moment, Emma thought he was going to faint. Then slowly, he recovered himself.

''John was a little tactless,'' he whispered. ''But that is passed. We have all recovered from my father's death. I thank you.'' And with that, holding himself stiffly erect, he spun upon his heel and left her.

Emma could have wept as she watched him hurriedly leave the crowd to seek a quiet place where he could be alone.

She had hurt him. She had never meant to hurt him. It was the last thing she had wanted. *You'll never know, Charles, how much I wanted to take your head upon my breast and stroke your curls and kiss you. You'll never know how much I wanted to take your pain away.*

I'm sorry, Charles, she apologized silently. *I wish I didn't keep . . . upsetting you. I love you, you know. I wish I could tell you. The trouble is, each time I try, my tongue seems to stick to the roof of my mouth.*

As she mused, Emma had drifted away from the others. Her feet had taken her to the room where she had been earlier with Lord Druce. The door was unlocked and she went in, finding, to her surprise, that John had come back here, too!

He did not see her. His back was to her, as was the back of his companion. The woman with Lord Druce must have found the room even more chilly than Emma had, for she was covered from head to foot in a voluminous purple cloak.

Emma was about to advance and make her presence known when she caught their words, and froze in her tracks.

"Why didn't you wait for me?"

"Wait for you? To do what, John?"

"To come back and marry you."

The woman laughed mockingly. "I would have grown into an old maid with waiting."

He looked as if she had struck him.

"It has been nearly three years, John," she reminded him. "I am not seventeen anymore. I am twenty. This year, I shall come of age. All my friends are married. I am the only one who is not, and I am their butt because of it."

"Then they are not friends. You should disown them."

The fair unknown snorted. "They have been more loyal to me than some I could name."

He clenched his hands. "This war will not last forever, and when it is over..."

"Don't you understand, John? I don't want to wait. I want to marry *now*—not at some distant date in the future, when I am old and withered and grey."

"My darling...can't you see? If I married you before the war is over, I...anything could happen. I—I might be killed...."

The other woman covered her face with her hands, and Emma's heart bled for her. *Poor lady!* Emma thought feelingly. *But who is she?*

The cloak obscured her form, and Emma did not recognize her voice. *I must not eavesdrop,* decided Emma, remembering her former Headmistresses' admonitions that a young lady never listens at keyholes like a servant.

"Ahem!" Emma cleared her throat, but Lord Druce and his lady were so engrossed in each other that they did not hear her.

Then, as she was about to speak again, Emma accidentally leaned against the wall. By the merest chance, her hand came into contact with a concealed catch, and the panelling opened as if by magic and swallowed her up.

Emma gave a horrified gasp. The wall had closed in on her. She was in a priest hole—one that must have been made for a very tall, thin priest, indeed!

"Help! Let me out!" she called.

"What's that?" asked the fair unknown.

"Just my guests playing games," replied Lord Druce, "Take no notice."

Emma stamped her feet with rage.

"Tears?" he questioned his companion.

"I cannot bear to think that you could be . . . killed."

"I'm sorry." He knelt at her feet. "I did not mean to distress you."

She ran her hands through his curls. "Oh, John! I wish—" Abruptly she stood up and walked away from him. Then, in a voice as flat as a fallen cake, she added, "It is too late for us now, anyway."

"No!" Lord Druce's protest was almost a scream.

Emma's hand fluttered to her breast as she felt his agony.

"Yes, it is. You know why. I am engaged."

A shudder passed through Lord Druce's frame. "Why did you have to become engaged to him? Why?

"We were seen together everywhere. People were beginning to talk. He had to propose. I had to accept."

Emma's eyebrows shot up.

Silly girl! she thought.

"And can you...go through with it?" asked Lord Druce.

"Certainly. He is wealthy. His family are well-connected. He is titled. What more could I want?"

"Love."

"Oh, John!" Her laugh was smothered by a sob. "Nobody marries for love these days. It is all positions, money and titles." She made as if to leave, and it was then Emma saw her face.

Lord Druce caught her hand. "Lavinia!"

Lord Brandford's betrothed was in love with Lord Druce!

"Oh, no!" whispered Emma.

CHAPTER SEVEN

FROM HER INVOLUNTARY concealment, Emma stared at Lavinia Smythe, whose countenance radiated pain and joy. Then her demeanor altered, and she returned to the demure, cool, perfect lady that Emma knew so well.

Lavinia loves John! Emma repeated silently. *Does Charles know?*

Instantly, she recalled the stricken, guilty expression that had flitted across Lord Druce's face a little earlier. Was it because of his love for Lavinia? wondered Emma. Did Charles suspect? Is that why he didn't want her to see John? Did he regard Lord Druce's presence as a threat to his own future with Lavinia Smythe?

If I saw John, mused Emma, *then I might inadvertently throw John and Lavinia together, and John would have a chance to court Lavinia. Is that it? Is Charles afraid I'll encourage them?*

A frown furrowed her brow. It was possible. And yet . . . inside her a tiny voice was telling her not to be such an idiot.

"No!" Lavinia Smythe was saying. "Let me go, John! It is too late for us. Don't you see?"

Lord Druce released her hand.

At once she hurried away to join the laughing, dancing throng.

Lord Druce hesitated for a moment. Then, suddenly, he was galvanized into action. "Lavinia!"

"John!" cried Emma as he rushed past the priest hole.

But Lord Druce either did not hear her or failed to understand her predicament.

What am I to do? Emma asked herself when she was left alone, cursing wretched priest holes, and wishing they had never been built! In frustration, she beat her hands upon the walls—without effect, for she remained a prisoner. *There must be some way out,* she told herself desperately.

IT TOOK HER THE BETTER PART of an hour's searching before she finally found the catch and released herself.

I must look a sight! she thought. Priest holes were not on the regular list of places to be cleaned; her hiding place had been dusty and filled with cobwebs.

Almost immediately, Emma ran into one of the maids, who stared, unabashed, at her dishevelled appearance.

"I have had a minor accident," explained Emma. "Please, can you take me somewhere where I may repair the damage?"

EMMA HAD NO SOONER RETURNED to the ballroom when Lord Druce approached.

"Emma! Where have you been? I have been looking up and down for you for at least an hour!"

Emma smiled and shrugged. "I had a slight mishap."

His concern was at once evident. "You are not hurt?"

"Oh, no. I merely became a little dusty. One of your maids very kindly brushed my gown. You see—" she whirled round to show him "—it is as good as new, isn't it?"

"Perfect!" He clasped her hand. "May I speak to you in private? There is something important I have to say...."

LORD DRUCE'S STUDY was in the west wing of The Rookery, far from the revelling crowds. Through its windows, Emma could see the illuminated terrace and the gardens, where some of the guests were walking to escape the excessive heat of the ballroom in the east wing.

Lord Druce placed the candelabra he had been carrying upon the walnut desk and drew the curtains. He offered Emma a red-and-white-striped chair, but she shook her head.

"Ahem! Emma..." he began awkwardly. "I have admired you for some time...."

Emma sat down smartly in the chair she had at first declined.

He is going to propose! she realized as he knelt before her. *I shall refuse, of course.* She could never marry a man who was in love with someone else!

Emma folded her hands in her lap and waited politely.

"I know you are fond of me...." he continued.

Emma could not deny it. She *was* fond of Lord Druce. She liked him very much... *But I don't love him!* she told herself.

"And I am very fond of you," proceeded Lord Druce.

Yes, that was true. He cared about her.... *But he does not love me,* she reminded herself.

"Emma, I..." Lord Druce threw caution to the winds. "Will you marry me?"

Within a split second, half a dozen replies went through Emma's mind.

She could tell him she was greatly honoured, but she must refuse. She could say, "Oh, this is so sudden! I cannot give you an answer now! I must have time to think!" She could tell him that her heart was given to another.

Wistfully, she conjured up a vision of the Earl of Brandford dancing with Lavinia.

It would open Lavinia's eyes if I were to accept John, she mused. They were so miserable apart. They would be so happy together. And if Lavinia thought she were about to lose Lord Druce to Emma... *Yet, if Lavinia leaves Charles for John,* Emma started to consider, *Charles will be so unbearably hurt....*

But would not the pain be far greater if Lord Brandford married Lavinia while she was still in love with Lord Druce?

Suddenly Emma smiled. "Yes, John." The words were out before she could stop them. "I should be honoured to become your wife."

Lord Druce clasped her hands and kissed them. "Emma, you have made me the happiest man in the world!" He sounded almost sincere.

He slipped a ruby ring onto Emma's fourth finger. It was much too large, and Emma recalled that Lavinia had plump fingers. Her own were much more slender.

"It is lovely!" she said aloud.

Lord Druce stared at her. A hot flush spread upwards from his ruff. He gulped as the ring slid up and down, refusing to settle.

"I, er, I shall have it made smaller—"

"Oh, no!" interrupted Emma. "Don't worry about it." It was at that moment that the door of the study burst open and Lord Brandford strode in.

"Charles," began Emma.

"How in the world...?" started Lord Druce.

"I saw you both from the terrace." The earl's gaze went coldly from Emma to Lord Druce, who was still on his knees before her. "Before you drew the curtains." As there was no response from either of his companions, he added, "May I ask what is going on?"

"Certainly, Charles!" Emma was all smiles. "John has proposed to me and I have accepted. We are to be married. I think in June—don't you, dear?"

Lord Druce nodded absently. "As you wish, my darling." His words did not carry conviction.

The Earl of Brandford's hands clenched at his sides. He stared at Emma with a strange, unfathomable expression that sent shivers along her spine.

"Er—aren't you going to congratulate us, Charles?" asked Lord Druce.

"Yes, of course, John," replied Lord Brandford.

It was the first time Emma had heard him use the other's Christian name, barring that one occasion when he had questioned her employment of it.

"My congratulations." His voice was flat and toneless.

Lord Druce stood up and they shook hands.

"My congratulations, Emma," added the earl. He stepped forward, seized Emma's hand and pressed it to his lips.

Emma tingled from head to foot. It was all she could do to stop herself from throwing herself in his arms.

Lord Brandford glanced at her fourth finger. His mouth curved down. "The ring is beautiful." He touched the glittering rubies. "A little large, though."

"We, er, are going to have it made smaller," said Lord Druce.

"But there is no need to rush. We have plenty of time." Emma bounced up from her chair, and seized Lord Druce by the hand. "We must tell the others!"

Lord Druce restrained her. "Just a minute, Emma! You are not thinking of making a public announcement?"

"Oh, no!" Emma's blond curls quivered at him. "That would be rather vulgar. I only thought that it would be nice to tell Lady Brandford, for it is she who introduced us. And Marcella. And Louis. And Lavinia."

Lord Druce swallowed. "Yes. I agree. I shall have the servants find them and . . . show them to one of my drawing rooms."

THEY WERE RANGED in an upper room hung with pewter damask. Lady Brandford looked quizzical, Lavinia seemed tense and Lady Marcella appeared puzzled—as did Louis de Troyes.

Lord Brandford's expression could not be seen. He was standing by the window, staring out at the rain falling in the darkness.

Lord Druce cleared his throat. "We have already told Charles, and we felt it would be...appropriate to gather you here to tell you. We, er, that is...Emma and I..."

"We are engaged!" exclaimed Emma with well-feigned ecstasy. "We are going to be married in June! Isn't it wonderful?"

Lavinia suddenly turned as pale as her Helen of Troy costume.

Lady Brandford's mouth tightened as her gaze went from her son to Emma, and Louis de Troyes looked stunned.

It was Lady Marcella who spoke first. "Oh, Emma, I'm so happy for you!" She flung her arms around her friend and kissed her. "And you, too, John!" Warmly she embraced him, as well.

"Yes." Louis de Troyes found his voice. "We are all very happy for you."

"You must show us the ring, Emma!" cried Lady Marcella.

Emma extended her left hand. She held on to the ring with her thumb so that no one would notice how it slipped and slid upon her finger. "Isn't it lovely?"

"Yes. It is exquisite," Lavinia managed in strangled tones. "My congratulations. I am sure you will be very happy together." Her blue eyes brimmed suddenly with tears.

Lord Druce went white.

"Excuse me." Lavinia dabbed at the tears with a handkerchief. "I'm crying. Isn't that silly? Weddings always make me cry. You're going to have a very foolish wife, Charles!''

As she fled from the room, Lady Brandford said, "Congratulations, Emma dearest. And you, too, John. Marcella, hadn't you better see to Lavinia?''

Lady Marcella departed at once, and her mother went on, "Charles, have you congratulated Emma and John?''

"Oh, yes. I have congratulated them...both.'' His face was ashen, as if he had suffered a mortal blow.

Emma felt guilty. *He has seen how Lavinia loves John!* she thought. *I have hurt him by showing him!* She hated herself for it.

"There is just one small point which worries me,'' murmured Lady Brandford. "Are you sure you are not rushing things? After all, you have not known each other very long.''

Emma shook her head vigorously. "There is no point in a long engagement. My father would not have stood for it. 'Plunge straight into battle.' That was his advice.''

Louis de Troyes arched his eyebrows. "I do hope, for your sake, Emma, that marriage will not be a battlefield.''

A titter of nervous laughter passed through the group.

IT WAS IN THE EARLY HOURS of the morning that Lady Brandford reentered the crimson salon at Brandford House.

"I am so angry I could spit!'' she declared. "How could John do this to us? And Emma! She must be out of her mind! She can't possibly marry him!''

"Lady Brandford, they are engaged.'' Louis de Troyes was blandly diplomatic. "What can one do?''

"Do? I know what I should like to do! I'd like to strangle the pair of them! Did you see the look on Charles's face?'' wept Lady Brandford. "I would like to throttle Lavinia into the bargain.'' She paced agitatedly up and down. Her sea-green Turkish robe swished across the par-

quet floor. "She ought never to have said yes to Charles."
She stopped and stared at her escort. "Why are you standing?"

"Because you are," replied Louis de Troyes.

Lady Brandford draped herself upon the sofa. "Why,"
she wailed as he pulled up an armchair, "did Charles have
to propose to Lavinia? Such folly! I could choke the life out
of him!"

Louis de Troyes wisely held his peace.

"And you..." accused Lady Brandford. "Why didn't you
stop them? I relied upon you to stop them!"

"Lady Brandford, there was nothing anyone could do.
These engagements came as a complete surprise...." He
flapped his hands, helplessly.

"Yes, I know." She sighed. "You are not to blame." And
then, she said more irritably, "But two more unsuited couples I have never in my life come across!"

"Calm yourself, Lady Brandford! It will do your heart no
good."

"My heart!" exclaimed Lady Brandford. "I knew there
was something I had forgotten. Now, where has Charles put
the whiskey?"

MEANWHILE, LAVINIA, MUFFLED in a capacious cloak with
a heavy veil concealing her features, had returned to The
Rookery.

Lord Druce had taken her into the study—the same study
where he had proposed to Emma. They were alone. The
servants were abed. The guests had all departed.

Gently, Lord Druce raised Lavinia's veil. He kissed her
cheek.

"My darling!" he murmured tenderly.

Lavinia's brilliant blue eyes met his hazel ones. "John,
you can't marry Emma!"

A mocking smile played about Lord Druce's lips. "Can't I, Lavinia? And what—or who—is to stop me?"

"John, Emma is a sweet, if awkward, young lady...."

"You have not always thought so."

"I know she has annoyed me in the past, but I—I can't help liking her...despite that."

"I am glad. It is nice to know that one's, er, friends will like one's wife."

"Oh, John! How can you possibly marry Emma? It is cruel to let her marry a man who is in love with another! You can't do that to her, John!"

Lord Druce studied his finely manicured fingernails. "Oh, Lavinia!" he replied in a bitter parody of her words. "How can you possibly marry Charles? It is cruel to let him marry a woman who is in love with another! You can't do that to him, Lavinia!"

Lavinia turned away from him. Anger was bubbling up inside her. "My engagement to Charles has nothing whatsoever to do with this!"

Lord Druce laughed mirthlessly. "Yes, it has. It has everything to do with this! You know it has!"

She made no reply.

"End your engagement to Charles," pleaded Lord Druce. "Say you'll marry me, and I'll break with Emma."

"I should be sued for breach of promise."

"I'll pay your damages, gladly."

"And your own damages? You could be sued for breach of promise too, John, if Emma has a mind to."

"I'll pay anything Charles or Emma ask. Even if it bankrupts me. It would be worth it to win you."

Lavinia swayed; then she steadied herself. "Why couldn't you have said this three years ago? It is too late now."

"It is not too late!"

"Yes, it is. Don't you see? I have given Charles my word. I cannot break it."

IN THE LIBRARY at Brandford House, the earl was pacing up and down. His eyes were dark and angry, his sensitive mouth twisted with rage.

"In spite of all I have said, you are going to marry John?"

"You have said nothing against him, Charles," returned Emma. "You know that. You are friends."

"He is unsuitable."

"He is charming, elegant, polite and titled."

"Bah!"

"He is careful of my honour."

"Careful of your honour!" fumed the earl. "He is going to marry you and you can say that?"

Emma blinked. "I do not see anything dishonourable about marriage."

The Earl bit back his reply, but not before Emma had seen a look of jealousy in his eyes.

Can it be? Is it possible? she asked herself excitedly. *Does Charles love* me?

Once more, a tiny flame of hope was ignited in her heart.

"M-marriage," the earl managed to respond, "is dishonourable if...if all things are not taken into account. There are some marriages that are...extremely dishonourable. There is dishonesty...on both sides."

"I have been perfectly frank with John," insisted Emma.

Lord Brandford was skeptical.

"At least," she amended, "I believe I have. Of course, I haven't told him how we met." She adjusted the folds of her Arcadian costume. "But since I couldn't see any bannisters which would bear sliding down at The Rookery, I thought it wouldn't matter."

Lord Brandford uttered a snort of exasperation.

"I don't know whether John has heard how I came to fall out of the window," continued Emma. "I can tell him about that before we marry, and about the other, er, accidents I have had, too. I'm sure he'll understand.''

Lord Brandford ground his teeth.

''John is very understanding.'' Emma smiled beatifically. ''So you see, there is no problem.''

''Emma, you shall not marry Lord Druce!'' ordered the earl. ''You shall break your engagement immediately!''

CHAPTER EIGHT

EMMA'S EYELASHES FLUTTERED provocatively. "I shall do nothing of the kind!"

"Emma," warned Lord Brandford, "you are playing with fire."

Instantly, Emma cast her eyes down. She was unaware, as she surveyed her black leather dancing pumps, of how much she was tempting him. Every gesture she made, from the quirk of her lips to the flicker of her eyelids seemed to say, "Take me."

Lord Brandford could not refuse her unspoken invitation. He seized hold of her and pressed his lips against hers.

Emma felt his passion searing her soul. The little flame of hope which had started to burn within her sprang to life. *He does love me!* she thought. Her desire became a roaring fire. She revelled in his kisses, responding with her own ardour. *Please say you love me, Charles!* she besought him soundlessly.

She did not know how long it lasted. But abruptly, outside in the street, a milkmaid called, "Milk! Fresh milk today!"

At once, Lord Brandford released Emma. He stared at her, and for a moment, she saw the hunger in his eyes. Then it vanished. His lips parted. He seemed about to say something.

Emma prepared for a sermon. He would tell her that she had behaved like a wanton; that she should remember she was engaged; that she should remember *he* was engaged.

But the words never came. Instead, the earl made her a low bow and without speaking, left the library.

"LOUIS!" LADY MARCELLA caught him just as he was about to leave Brandford House.

"Yes, my darling?"

"Come into the dining room." She fairly dragged him in.

The room was still curtained. Lady Marcella lit a candle. It seemed incongruous as the early-morning rays of the sun shone through the gaps in the apple-green shutters.

"What is it, Marcella?"

Lady Marcella frowned. "I don't know how to say this, but . . . Louis, are they going to be happy?"

"Who?"

"Emma and John."

Louis de Troyes shrugged. "If they love each other . . ."

"But do they?"

Another shrug. "I don't know." He paused. "Are Lavinia and Charles in love?"

"No."

Louis de Troyes sighed.

Lady Marcella made a face. She seated herself on an armchair upholstered in oyster satin. "Charles has turned into a perfect—" she searched frustratedly for the right word "—a perfect icicle. There are times when I feel I would like to light a fire under him, just to thaw him out a little."

Louis de Troyes's mouth twitched. He opened his arms and Lady Marcella flew into them. As they surfaced from their embrace, he remarked, "I have noticed that Charles is cooler than usual. It is as if he is trying to hide his emotions. He is almost like a prisoner before he goes to be tortured."

"What a horrible thing to say, Louis!"

"I am sorry. I was thinking aloud. It had not occurred to me before. But now that you mention it . . ."

"Hmm. Yes," returned Lady Marcella as his voice trailed away. "There is something wrong. I feel it and it is worrying me."

"I feel it, too." He took her hand and kissed it.

"I wish Charles and Lavinia weren't going to marry," murmured Lady Marcella. "I wish Emma and John weren't going to marry. I wish *we* were going to marry instead!"

Louis de Troyes smiled. "Shall we elope to Gretna Green? We shall not be missed for at least twelve hours."

Lady Marcella laughed happily. "Oh, Louis! What a wonderful idea! I would love to do it! But you know what would happen. Mother dear will be upset—and Charles would be impossible!"

"So we must wait."

"Alas, yes!"

"Ah! What a pity!"

Lady Marcella shot him a sideways look. "You had better go, Louis, before I decide not to wait!"

IN THE DAYS THAT FOLLOWED, an unnatural calm reigned.

Lord Druce called frequently upon Emma. As a lover should, he brought her gifts: a silver basket for posies of flowers; a diamond star for her hair; a pair of lemon-yellow gloves.

The Earl of Brandford was pursuing the same course with Lavinia Smythe. He presented her with a fine ermine tippet; a gold lorgnette for the theatre; a silver watch upon a chain to wear about her waist.

Meanwhile, Lady Brandford gave teas, dinners and suppers where the happy couples were received with studied politeness. The wedding arrangements were discussed. Everyone was in total agreement on every single point.

Such tranquility could not last. It was exceptional: like the lull before the storm.

ONE MORNING, LORD DRUCE came to call upon Emma. He asked after her health. He enquired about everyone else at Brandford House.

Emma answered his questions. She told him that she had received a letter from Miss Foxall and Miss Quince, not to mention half a dozen missives from her friends at the Houghton Academy.

As expected, Lord Druce commented upon the letters, but in such a detached manner that Emma thought, *This is not like John!*

"Is anything the matter?" she queried.

He glanced at her and bit his lip. "Emma, I—" He halted, then, after drawing a deep breath, he began again. "I went to Carlton House last night. The Prince Regent sent for me."

"How wonderful!" exclaimed Emma. "It must be a great honour."

Lord Druce inclined his head. "His Royal Highness wished me to undertake an assignment."

"And you agreed?"

"Yes. I—"

"Marvelous!" Emma kissed him. "To be doing something for the Prince Regent, for England. I am so proud of you!"

Lord Druce blushed. "I...I thank you." He did not smile. His face was grim. He fidgeted nervously, as if he did not know how to proceed. "My assignment will take me... abroad. I—I shall have to travel through France...."

France! France was ruled by Napoleon Bonaparte, the emperor. The United Kingdom was at war with France, and had been for many years.

Emma's rapturous smile faded. "You will be in danger?"

"Yes."

"How serious is it?"

"I don't wish to alarm you."

"My father was a soldier. I am accustomed to such things."

"I—I may not . . . come back."

"Oh, John!" Her hands reached out to clasp his.

She held them only a moment, for he withdrew almost instantly from her. She let him move across the room. The light from the window illuminated half his face and she saw the strain etched upon his usually cheerful features.

"Is there anything I can do?" offered Emma.

Lord Druce swallowed a soundless sob. With difficulty he spoke once more, "I—I hate to have to ask you this, but would you mind if we . . . ended our engagement?"

Emma was very still.

"If you are engaged to me," Lord Druce stumbled on, "or if we were married and . . . something happened to me, you would suffer. A second marriage, a second engagement, would be hard to accomplish."

He was right. Widows—and women whose betrotheds had died before they were married—had not much chance of finding a second partner. Miss Foxall and Miss Quince had impressed that upon Emma when they had told her their own stories.

Emma twisted her handkerchief in her hands. "Have you mentioned this to anyone else?"

"No. No one. Only you. You—you had a right to know."

"Hmm." Emma cast her blue eyes down. "You have not said anything to Lavinia?"

"Lavinia!" Surprise, shock and consternation were in his voice. "No! Of course not! Why—why on earth should I tell Lavinia?"

"Because you are in love with her."

"In love with her?" He forced himself to laugh. "What an extraordinary notion! I—"

Emma removed his ring from the chain that hung around her neck. She handed it to him. "Don't deny it. It is Lavinia whom you really love. It is Lavinia for whom this ring was originally made. It is Lavinia whom you really wish to marry."

Lord Druce flushed to the roots of his light brown hair. "I—I..." His hazel eyes widened. He stared at her. "How—how long have you known?"

"Do you remember when I told you I had a slight mishap at your masquerade?"

"I remember."

"I fell into a priest hole. It was while you and Lavinia were talking to each other. You had your backs to me, so you did not see me enter. I called out, I tried to make you aware...." Emma's shoulders lifted. "I heard everything."

"Oh, thank heavens!" Lord Druce sank on one knee before her. His head was in his hands. "I have felt such a bounder. I should never have proposed to you. I was hurt, and I wanted to lash out at Lavinia. I—I was a fool. I have not had a moment's peace since, Emma. I was terrified that you would find out and that it would cause you dreadful pain...."

"Poor John!" murmured Emma sympathetically. "I didn't mean you to suffer. I knew you did not love me when you asked for my hand. I knew you loved Lavinia. I ought to have refused you, but I wanted to help. I thought that if I accepted your proposal, it would make Lavinia angry, and she would break her engagement with Charles, and you would be brought together again."

Lord Druce raised his head and looked earnestly at her. "Emma, is this true?"

Emma nodded. She tried to look contrite. "I shouldn't have done it. I am so sorry. Miss Foxall and Miss Quince would have been very angry with me, if they had known."

"Angry? Why on earth...?"

She sighed. "I've got into so many scrapes, you see. And now that I am nineteen—nearly twenty," she amended, "I ought to know better."

He frowned.

"And I should have thought of Charles," she said.

"Charles! Gracious!" he spluttered.

"Actually—" Emma put her head to one side "—I did think of Charles. I was worried that he might be hurt."

"So he might! He . . ."

"Yes." She prevented him from saying more. "He might well be hurt if Lavinia left him for you. But I felt he would be far more hurt if he married her when she did not love him—especially if he found out later." She worried her lower lip with her teeth. "Even so, I shouldn't have interfered."

"No, no. You were right." Lord Druce covered her hands with kisses. "Oh, may heaven bless you, Emma!"

Emma regarded him cautiously. "You are not making fun of me, are you?"

"Goodness, no! I cannot tell you what a weight you have taken off my mind." He sprang to his feet. His former zest for life had returned. He was almost his old jaunty self.

"Do you mean that?"

"With all my heart!" He folded his arms across his chest. "I was so afraid that I had deceived you. You do not know how I cursed myself for my folly. I knew I should not have asked you for your hand in marriage. But Lavinia's rejection . . ."

"I know," Emma reminded him. "I heard." She looked up at him. "We can still be friends?"

"Of course, Emma. I shall always be your friend. And I hope you will be mine." He extended his hand and she shook it solemnly.

"I should like nothing better." She met his gaze frankly. "But our engagement is finished?"

"It is better so."

"I agree."

He coughed. "You may—ahem—keep my gifts."

"Oh, no. I shall return—"

"Please don't. I meant them in friendship."

"You are very kind, John."

"Not at all." He hesitated. "And Emma...there is one thing you can do for me...."

"What is it?"

"Please don't tell Lavinia about this."

"About what?" asked Emma innocently.

"My going to the Continent."

Emma grimaced.

"You were going to tell her, weren't you?"

Emma nodded guiltily. "I thought..."

"You thought it would bring her to my side?"

"Yes."

"It will not. Her pride—her deuced pride!—will see to that!"

"But..."

He shook his head, silencing her. "I am leaving very soon. Lavinia will not come to my side if she knows the danger I am in, but she will worry and fret. It is her way. The burden will be too much for her. She will sink into a decline. And I...." His voice was hoarse with emotion. "I shall be torn to pieces knowing how she will suffer. So please, I beg you, say nothing."

"She shall not learn of it from me, I promise you."

"Thank you, Emma!" His relief was plain to see.

"There is one thing I should like to ask of you, John."

"What is it?"

"That we keep the fact that we have broken our engagement a secret—between ourselves—for the moment."

Lord Druce frowned. "Are you sure?"

"I am sure."

"Very well." He glanced at the clock. "Excuse me, I must go now. I have preparations to make."

LORD DRUCE HAD FINISHED attending to a host of last-minute details. His horse had been saddled. The groom had been sent for to bring it to the front door. In a few moments, he would be travelling south to the coast, where a Royal Navy frigate was waiting for him. He had his passport in his hand when the doors of his study were flung wide.

"Miss Lavinia Smythe!" announced his butler.

Lord Druce wheeled round. His face was white. He fought to control his agitation.

Lavinia, in a charming eggshell-blue pelisse trimmed with mink, swept in. Smilingly, she extended her hand to him. "John! How are you?"

"How are you?" he countered, kissing her fingertips.

His eyes watched her like a hawk's.

Has Emma broken her word? he wondered bitterly. *Or has someone else told Lavinia?*

Lavinia studied him closely. "Is something the matter? You look a little pale."

"I am fine, I assure you." With an effort, he made himself smile. His heart stopped pounding so wildly.

She doesn't know! he realized. *I misjudged Emma!*

"What brings you here?" he asked.

Lavinia answered with a little laugh. "I wanted to invite you to come to the theatre with us on Tuesday. A private theatrical, actually. We are having a performance of Sheridan's *The Rivals*. We have hired the Hartshorne Theatre in the Strand. It has been entirely redecorated and reopens officially the day after. We even have Master Betty in the play. Do say you will come."

"I—I won't be able to."

"Oh? Why not?"

"I, uh, am going on a...trip." He ran his hand nervously through his hair. "I can't say how long it will take."

Lavinia was disappointed. "But if you are back in time, will you come?"

"Yes. Certainly." It was at that moment that Lord Druce accidently let his passport slip through his fingers. It fell onto the floor.

Lavinia, seeing it at her feet, instinctively stooped to pick it up. "Here." She was in the process of restoring it to Lord Druce when her eye fell on the strange script, and she gasped. "John!" she cried accusingly. "This is a French passport!"

Lord Druce seized it hastily from her. "You are mistaken." He rammed it into his breast pocket.

"I am not mistaken! I have seen that style of lettering before. And I know what a French passport looks like. We were in France during the Peace of Amiens. Remember?"

Lord Druce was silent.

Lavinia grasped the lapels of his grey overcoat. "John! That is a French passport! I know it! What are you doing with a French passport?"

"Lavinia, please..." He tried to remove her hands, but she clung more tightly.

There was a loud knock at the door.

"That means my horse is saddled," he informed Lavinia.

"No!" she whispered.

"I shall be with you in a moment!" he called.

"John!"

"Forgive me, Lavinia," he said softly. "I must leave you now. I cannot delay."

Lavinia's hands dropped to her side. "You are going to France!"

He did not answer.

Her face had drained of colour. Her eyes were large, dark pools of misery. "You cannot go to France, John! You cannot!"

"Lavinia!" Tenderly his fingers caressed her cheek. "Calm yourself. I am only going on a short journey."

"Where?"

"To the south coast."

"Where on the south coast?"

"Sandwich." The Royal Navy frigate was waiting for him there.

"And after Sandwich?" she persisted.

He smiled sadly and shook his head. "Don't worry, my darling. I'll be back again before you know it."

EMMA LED A WEEPING LAVINIA down the stairs. She had just seen her into her carriage when Lord Brandford appeared in the hallway, blocking her path. His face was sombre.

"Good morning, Charles." Emma smiled brightly at him and tried to walk around him.

He gripped her arm. "Emma, I would like a word with you."

Oh, dear! thought Emma. *What have I done now?*

"Certainly, Charles," she responded, while feverishly racking her brains for the answer.

They went into the study.

Emma sat down on one of the burgundy velvet chairs, with her hands folded in her lap. She felt much the same as she had when she was about to be severely reprimanded by Miss Foxall and Miss Quince.

Lord Brandford leaned against the study doors, using the weight of his body to shut them behind him. "Did I see you hand Lavinia into her carriage?"

"You did."

"Was she crying?"

"Yes."

A black thundercloud settled upon his countenance. "What in the world did you say to upset her?"

"*I* didn't upset her!"

"Then why was she crying?"

Emma cast her innocent blue eyes down. She sighed feelingly. "She went to see John, to invite him to a theatrical evening..."

"And?"

"She discovered he is going to France."

"*What!*"

Emma, unnerved by his roar, leapt up from her place.

Lord Brandford's hands landed heavily upon her shoulders, pushing her back again. "What do you mean?"

"I mean exactly what I say, Charles! And please take your hands off me—you are hurting me."

Lord Brandford released her instantly. "Going to France? John?" he echoed incredulously.

"On a mission for the Government, at the request of the Prince Regent."

Lord Brandford assessed her. "You...knew?"

"Of course I knew!"

"And you did nothing to stop him?"

Emma closed her eyes and communed with her soul. When she and her soul had finished discussing the matter, she opened her eyes again.

"John was determined to go." She repeated almost word for word what she had said to Lavinia. "I could not hold him back. All I could do was give him my complete support."

Lord Brandford banged his fist on the desk. "Why wasn't I told?"

Emma stood up. "Because," she retorted crossly, "it was none of your business." She turned and prepared to walk out of the room.

Lord Brandford, with three swift strides, overtook her and planted himself in front of her. "We have not finished."

"*You* have not finished. *I* have!"

"Emma—" His voice was tightly controlled. "Would you please have the goodness to sit down and listen to what I have to say?"

Emma walked back to the chair she had just vacated. She sat, but the rigidity of her body made her resistance plain.

Lord Brandford took a deep breath to steady himself. "If John is really going to France . . ." he began in level, steady tones.

"He is," interposed Emma.

"He could be killed."

"I realize that."

"That would leave you, as his fiancée, in an invidious position."

Emma tilted her head enquiringly.

"You must break your engagement to John."

Emma stared at him.

Oh, horrors! she thought. *Whatever am I to say?*

"I—I c-can't," she stammered.

"You can't? Why not?"

Emma licked her lips. "We, er, we settled all that before he left. I could not possibly change things now."

"Of course you can!" countered the earl. "My horses can outrun his any day. It is a simple matter of knowing which direction he is going in, writing him a letter and sending it with a messenger."

"No."

Lord Brandford's lips were set in a thin angry line. "I know John very well. I am sure that he must have asked you to break your engagement."

Emma looked extremely guilty.

"He did, didn't he?"

"Yes," she confessed.

"And you refused?"

She was silent.

"Oh, you little idiot!" He paced up and down, scarcely troubling to conceal his exasperation. "For his sake—if not for your own—you must break your engagement! It would be better for all concerned!"

Emma gave him her penitent-nun expression. Miss Foxall and Miss Quince would not have been taken in by it. They were only too well aware that young ladies who contrive to look like penitent nuns are usually concealing something. Lord Brandford, however, did not have their long experience with the fair sex.

"You are mistaken, Charles." Emma's voice throbbed with emotion. "You cannot imagine how mistaken! You do not know what you are asking!"

Then with the air of a tragic heroine, she rose slowly and gracefully to her feet and floated out of the study.

Lord Brandford clenched his hands. As far as he was concerned, there could be only one reason for her behaviour.

She loves John so passionately, he assumed, that if he dies, she will not marry another.

His brain told him he ought to applaud her single-minded devotion.

So why did his heart feel as if it had been tossed in amongst the thorns?

CHAPTER NINE

IT HAD BEEN SEVERAL WEEKS since Lord Druce's departure for the Continent. Winter had passed, and a wet February had heralded the arrival of spring. The daffodils had been and gone; the trees were beginning to blossom.

Neither Lavinia Smythe nor the Earl of Brandford had seen fit to alter their wedding date; it was still to be on the last Saturday in May.

"Beast! Wretch!" Emma hissed at his lordship's portrait, which seemed to look down at her from its lavishly carved frame with a supercilious air, much like the subject himself. *It's not glad to see me back,* mused Emma, *and neither is he!*

She had been in the country visiting Lord Druce's family. He had more cousins, she had discovered, than King George III had bibles. Now she was in London once more, and Lady Brandford had invited her to stay. Naturally, she had accepted the invitation, reflecting that her ladyship was kind to take such an interest in her.

It was as well that Emma did not know why Lady Brandford had asked her to Brandford House again; it would have made her self-conscious. The fact was, her ladyship had been trying to prevent her son from marrying Lavinia. So far, her efforts had met with no success, but she was still hopeful—hence her invitation to Emma, which was in essence another bid to stop the wedding.

Emma, still wearing her salmon-pink mantle over her cambric travelling dress, was about to mount the magnificent staircase when, behind her, Wooster, the butler, coughed discreetly.

Emma turned. "Yes, Wooster?"

"There is a person to see you, Miss Armstead."

"A person?"

"A person," reiterated Wooster. His tone conveyed his contempt, and Emma felt that he could not have been more displeased if he had found a mouse in his oxtail soup.

"Does this person have a name?"

"This person has no name, but desires to speak with you regarding an urgent matter." There was more than hint, in Wooster's voice, that whatever the nameless one's business was, it was bound to be unsavory.

Emma frowned, then curiosity got the better of her. Airily, she said, "Well, I suppose I had better find out what is wanted. Where do you suggest I receive this person?"

Wooster sniffed. He would have suggested that she *not* receive this person, but it was not his place to correct a guest of Lady Brandford. "One might consider receiving him in the conservatory, Miss Armstead."

The conservatory was outside Brandford House. It could be reached from the house by her ladyship and her guests. It also possessed a servants' door and a tradesmen's entrance.

"The conservatory it is." Emma untied her bonnet and mantle and passed them to her maid. "Would you please show this person there?"

EMMA WAS ALREADY SEATED amidst Lady Brandford's delicate and sheltered plants when Wooster ushered in a man who looked as if he had once been a sailor.

His face was weatherbeaten, his eyes small, closely set and bright. His jacket was worn and patched, his shirt almost threadbare and his trousers wide and baggy. He wore no shoes, and he stank. There were no two ways about it. He stank.

Emma gave no sign of offence. She smiled welcomingly. "I'm Emma Armstead. And you are?"

"A friend," he growled.

Emma's eyebrows arched. *Most peculiar!* she thought. Then, still smiling, she asked, "Would you like something to drink?"

"I would."

"A glass of, er, rum?"

"I wouldn't say no."

"A glass of rum for my friend, if you please, Wooster, and a sherry for me."

Wooster looked pained. "Very good, Miss Armstead."

He went to fulfil her wishes and returned promptly with a glass of rum and a glass of sherry borne high upon a silver tray. He set them down on the round white table between Emma and her guest. Then he bowed and absented himself.

Emma clinked glasses with her strange companion, then waited for him to speak, sipping her sherry. He drank his rum. He was almost half way down the glass when he decided the time had come.

"I was told you'd give me ten pound."

Emma was taken aback. "Ten pounds?" It was more than some people earned in a year. Yet this ragged wretch, who chopped and changed the English language to suit himself, had suddenly demanded such a sum.

"Ten pound," he repeated obstinately.

Reflecting that there had to be a reason, Emma ventured, "May I ask who..."

"John Druce."

For a moment, Emma did not recognize the name, shorn of its title. Then the light dawned.

"Ah! He sent you with a message for me?"

"A friend" nodded.

"In that case, I shall certainly give you your money." Emma summoned Wooster once more and sent him to fetch the requisite amount for her. The butler, who seemed to view the whole transaction with grave misgivings, returned in a short time with the money.

When he had departed again, Emma placed the ten pounds on the table in front of her. Her guest made as if to seize it, but Emma put her hand firmly over it.

"The message?"

"Aye. He's a prisoner."

Emma gasped and lifted her hand. "A prisoner? Of the French?"

"Aye," agreed her companion. "I had a chance to 'scape. I took it. He give me some French money...."

"Couldn't he join you?"

"A friend" smiled grimly. "Not a hope. He was in irons. But he give me the money. 'There's ten pound for you,' said he, 'if you take a letter to Miss Emma Armstead, what lives at the Earl of Brandford's house in the west end of London, beyond Piccadilly.' Man of his word. A gentleman, that John Druce."

So saying, he removed a letter from his shirt pocket and pushed it across the table to Emma.

"AHEM!" WOOSTER WAS FAMED for his ominous coughs.

Although the Earl of Brandford was in the middle of removing his riding clothes, the butler's portent attracted his attention immediately.

"Yes, Wooster?"

"I beg your pardon, my lord...but there is a matter which I would like to bring before you...."

The earl's enquiring expression did not change as he made a sign to dismiss his valet.

"Yes? What is it, Wooster?"

"I hope your lordship will not think me impertinent...."

"Never."

"I should not wish to lose your lordship's good opinion...."

"There is no likelihood of your so doing."

"Normally, I would say nothing...."

"Quite."

"But I feel that it is my duty to apprise you of the circumstances...."

"Exactly."

Wooster folded his hands behind his back. He rocked uneasily on his heels. He cleared his throat. Then, at last he pronounced, "It concerns Miss Armstead."

Lord Brandford was suddenly very alert. "Ye-e-es?"

"She has received *a person*."

"What kind of a person?"

"A person of an inferior social standing."

"I see." Lord Brandford pursed his lips. "Naturally, she is at liberty to receive whomever she wishes."

"Quite so, my lord. But—ahem!—she has given this person a sum of money."

"Has this person done some work for her?"

"I think not, my lord. She does not seem to have been previously acquainted with him."

"Yet she welcomed him?"

"She—" Wooster shuddered at the memory "—she asked me to serve him a glass of rum...and herself a glass of sherry."

Lord Brandford's sensitive features clouded. "Pray continue."

"I fear—though of course I may be completely mistaken—that this person is attempting to, er, blackmail Miss Armstead."

Lord Brandford's mouth tightened. "I see. Thank you, Wooster. You have done well."

Wooster bowed.

"I shall deal with the matter."

"Very good, my lord."

"Does anyone else know about this, er, person?"

"No one, your lordship."

"I may rely upon your discretion?"

"I have forgotten the incident already."

"Excellent, Wooster!"

EMMA HAD DISCARDED her travelling attire and changed into a fresh muslin gown embroidered with daisies and buttercups. She had just entered the sitting room adjoining her bedroom, when the Earl of Brandford burst in.

Caught by surprise, Emma dropped her saffron-yellow reticule onto the carpet. Half a dozen items fell, scattering here, there and everywhere.

Lord Brandford and Emma spent the next five minutes looking for farthings, smelling salts, a scent bottle, a bit of sealing wax and other tiny, eminently crushable objects which had rolled into the most inconvenient places.

"I think that is everything," remarked Emma, as she picked up a porcelain button.

She was crouched under a square, inlaid table, gazing straight into Lord Brandford's eyes.

"Good." He, like her, was on his hands and knees. "Because I want to talk to you."

"Oh, really? What about?"

"Your visitor."

"My...?" For a moment Emma's large blue eyes were completely blank. Then the penny dropped. "Oh. Him. He's gone."

"You paid him some money."

Emma grimaced. "I suppose Wooster told you that."

"It is of no consequence. It will not go any farther."

"Hrmph!"

"How much did you pay him?"

Emma squirmed. "Well . . . he wanted ten pounds . . . but I actually gave him twenty. He—he had no shoes, you see . . ." Her voice trailed away.

"Is he blackmailing you?"

Emma burst out laughing. "No, of course not! What on earth could he blackmail me about?"

"I haven't the faintest idea." Lord Brandford was fighting for control. "May one ask why you paid him money?"

"Certainly. He brought me a letter from John."

The Earl of Brandford stiffened, and forgetting where he was, he succeeded in hitting his head on the underside of the table.

"Ow!" Manfully, he suppressed a string of military oaths and massaged his scalp tenderly.

Emma made a mental note to be more careful when *she* stood up.

"Oh, dear. Is it very painful?"

"No." Lord Brandford silently cursed himself for being a fool.

"Would you like some ice?"

"No, er, thank you." He edged out from under the table and rose to his feet. "And how is John?"

"Not very well. He has been captured by the French." Emma was on her feet now, too. "They put him in irons."

A small strangled cry caused them both to turn.

Lavinia Smythe was standing in the doorway. Lady Marcella was behind her.

"Oh!" exclaimed Lady Marcella. "I didn't realize . . . you had company. I—I thought . . ."

"It's all right. Come in," invited Emma.

Lavinia, deathly white, hands outstretched, stumbled forward. "John...captured by the French...and...in irons?"

"It sounds worse than it is," comforted Emma. "He's not in irons anymore. At least he won't be in a day or two." She cleared her throat. "He had a message for you, Lavinia."

"What...is it?"

"He begs you..." Emma began, then quoted Lord Druce's own words, "'if you have any feelings for me whatsoever, that you will never marry for any reason but love.'"

At these words, Lavinia uttered a heartrending cry and collapsed in a heap at Lady Marcella's feet.

"Now see what you have done!" raged the Earl of Brandford.

Emma, at whom his fury was directed, sniffed offendedly and stalked out of the room.

EMMA CONSIDERED THE MATTER all night. By morning, she was firmly resolved that John had to be rescued.

There were several reasons for her decision: to begin with, Lord Druce was a friend. Whenever friends were in trouble, they had to be helped. Furthermore, Lord Druce was in love with Lavinia, and he wanted to marry her. And he could hardly do that if he were in a French gaol, now could he?

Not only that, but Lavinia, too, was a friend. Lord Druce's captivity was making her dreadfully unhappy. The best way to cheer her up would be to secure his release.

Besides which, Lavinia was in love with Lord Druce. She wanted to marry him. True, she had not admitted it publicly yet, but Emma knew that if anything should happen to Lord Druce while he was in prison, Lavinia would die of grief. That would not do.

"John has to be rescued!" declared Emma aloud. Her resolution formed, Emma next devoted herself to the practical task of making it a reality. "Who is going to rescue John?" she asked herself.

Lavinia, though she had a great many excellent qualities, was simply not capable of it. Lord Brandford, while capable of it, had shown no inclination to undertake the task.

Louis de Troyes, being an émigré, would be in too much danger. If he so much as set foot on French soil, he might forfeit his life. With such a threat hanging over him, he could hardly be expected to have pretensions in that direction.

One by one, Emma went through the list of her acquaintances, and one by one, she discarded them. Eventually, she concluded that since no one else seemed likely to attempt this enterprise ... *she* would.

"The first step," reckoned Emma, "is to get a boat." After all, one could scarcely order one's carriage to drive across the Channel.

It occurred to Emma that the person most likely to be able to produce a vessel of some kind was the Earl of Brandford. So, as soon as she was dressed, she went to find him.

He was not at Brandford House. He had, she learned, "gone out" and would not be back "until later." She considered that it was extremely inconsiderate of him. *Who will know where he has gone?* wondered Emma. *Ah! Wooster!* She summoned the butler.

"Wooster, please can you tell me where Lord Brandford is this morning?"

"His lordship is in the City."

The City of London. The original one square mile. The venerable, ancient and compact part of the now-sprawling metropolis.

"At what address?" asked Emma.

Wooster's composure was shaken.

The City was not a fashionable resort. Furthermore, it was a male preserve. No lady—certainly no lady who was a guest of Lady Brandford's—would dream of visiting the City.

In all his life, Wooster had never heard of anyone with social aspirations travelling further east than Charing Cross, unless of course, they had a particular reason—like Lord Brandford. Exceptions had to be made somewhere.

"Lord Brandford will be at the offices of Messrs. Dapp and Hisscoke. They are accountants. They reside in Saxon Lane, off Cheapside." His tone indicated the undesirability of calling at these premises.

Emma beamed at him. "Thank you, Wooster. Will you order a carriage for me, please?"

Wooster looked as if the end of the world had come. Valiantly, he strove to stave off disaster. "Lord Brandford will be seeing several people." He coughed behind a white-gloved hand. "They may not be, er, gentlemen."

Emma's blue eyes fastened trustingly on him.

"There will be no ladies present," persisted Wooster. "And no women, either."

"Oh, I don't mind," said Emma. "Miss Foxall and Miss Quince taught me that I must be prepared to deal with all manner of people."

There was a sharp intake of breath from Wooster. He made one final effort. "You may be obliged to wait in . . . most uncomfortable conditions."

Emma's countenance remained seraphic. "Miss Foxall and Miss Quince taught me to bear my lot with equanimity, however distasteful it may be."

Wooster, shattered, went to order the carriage.

EMMA HAD TO LEAVE the carriage in Cheapside, Saxon Lane being too narrow for anything other than a pedestrian. She soon located the premises of Messrs. Dapp & Hisscoke in a dingy building, four stories high, that leaned unsteadily against its neighbor.

Emma was ushered into a drab, narrow room lined with hard wooden benches. A number of Messrs. Dapp and Hisscoke's clients were waiting their turns there. They were clean, but poorly dressed, in varying shades of grey and black with, here and there, a shiny brass or mother-of-pearl button visible.

They were, as Wooster had warned her, merely men. No gentlemen. No ladies. And no women.

They were all immensely bored. Some of them were staring up at the ceiling, some were asleep, and one was snoring. It was a quiet snore, like a kettle continually boiling on the hearth. One or two were reading newspapers. One was frowning worriedly as he perused a lengthy document.

Emma did a quick calculation. About thirty of them, she guessed. If each of them takes five minutes, that means . . . two and a half hours! Emma sat down and prepared to be patient.

The room in which they were sitting was hot and stuffy. The more Emma thought about it, the more she wished she had not put on her stockings. *They are so very warm!* she mused. *I do wish I had left them off!* Just a pair of pumps would have been much more comfortable.

Emma glanced around her. Usually when she entered a room, someone smiled at her or bowed or admired her beauty. But not one of these men had taken the slightest notice of her. True, her shining blond curls were hidden under a plain straw bonnet, and she was wearing a simple blue gingham dress. But even so, one of them might at least have doffed his hat to her!

She studied them more closely. *They are all so old!* observed Emma to herself. *Ten thousand years together, I shouldn't wonder!* She sighed again. *I don't suppose anybody would mind if I took off my stockings,* she reflected.

They were not full-length stockings. They only came up to her calves.

No, of course, they won't mind! she told herself. They won't even notice. I'll be very discreet. No one will be the wiser.

Emma leaned forward, and her hand crept down her right leg. Gently, she removed her pump. Gracefully—and cautiously—she slid her hand up her right leg as far as her calf. She unbuckled her garter and pulled it, and her right stocking, quickly down. Daintily she wriggled out of her stocking. It came off quite easily, and it was such a relief.

What bliss! thought Emma, as she stuffed the stocking and the garter into her reticule.

"WHAT ARE YOU DOING?" demanded the Earl of Brandford.

Whicks, the most junior member of Messrs. Dapp & Hisscoke, straightened, and a deep red flush of embarrassment spread over his freckled face. Even his ears burned.

"This, er, this lock...it was...stiff..." he mumbled awkwardly.

Lord Brandford bent down and peered through the large keyhole. The first person his gaze fell upon was Emma. She was in the process of removing her left stocking.

He nearly had apoplexy.

CHAPTER TEN

EMMA PUSHED THE SECOND STOCKING and its garter into her reticule, feeling much cooler. She was extremely pleased with herself... until she glanced up.

Lord Brandford had moved swiftly and soundlessly across the carpeted floor. He was standing directly in front of her, his face as black as thunder.

Emma gulped. *What have I done?* she wailed silently.

Apprehensively, she glanced about her. Thirty pairs of eyes were upon her, their expressions ranging from mildly interested to positively lecherous. Not a single one of the men was decently asleep now—or bored!

And I was so careful! reflected Emma crossly. *And so quiet!* The tips of her stockings were still hanging over the top of her reticule. She packed them firmly in, then smiled up at the earl.

"Good morning."

"Good morning," he snapped from between clenched teeth. "Would you please step this way?"

Emma did not dare to mention that she was not first in the queue, and no one else, seeing the earl's expression, had the courage to remark upon it.

Lord Brandford escorted Emma through a maze of offices, past curious articled clerks to a tiny, private, inner chamber. There he seated her in a large, sturdy chair, and leaned over her, putting his hands upon its arms. His brown eyes crackled with anger.

"What," he snarled at her, "do you mean by exposing yourself in this office?"

Emma glared back at him. "I did not expose myself. I merely removed my stockings."

"You revealed your ankles!"

"I did not! My toes were scarcely visible!"

"It was not your toes that attracted an enchanted audience of no less than thirty men!"

"If they had been gentlemen, they would have averted their eyes!"

A muscle in Lord Brandford's cheek began to throb. Slowly, deliberately, he moved out of striking range. He glanced down at his hands and saw to his amazement that they were shaking uncontrollably. He decided to change the subject.

"May one ask what brought you here in the first place?"

"Certainly." Emma was relieved that she was not to be scolded any more. "I came to ask you if you had a boat, and if so, may I borrow it?"

"A boat?"

"Yes. A vessel for sailing in."

"Do you mean a ship?"

"Oh, a ship, by all means, if you like."

Lord Brandford was suspicious. "Why?"

"The sea air is so salubrious...." Emma was proud of herself for remembering the word. She had misspelled it three times in her English lessons, and forgotten the definition. Now at last she had both right. "...at this time of year. A trip on the waves would be beneficial to my health."

Lord Brandford's brown eyes narrowed almost to slits. "Why couldn't you have waited until I came home this evening to ask me?"

Emma cast round for a suitable reply.

Why is she dithering? wondered the earl for a moment, then, all at once, he divined the cause of her hesitation.

"No!" he said firmly.

"No?" Emma was disappointed.

"Under no circumstances."

"Not at all?"

"No!" he repeated.

"Not even a tiny little boat?" She indicated the size with her thumb and forefinger.

"No!"

Emma sulked. "It is very hot," she observed. "That is why I had to remove my stockings, and—"

"Don't try to pull the wool over my eyes, Emma Armstead!" interrupted Lord Brandford. "I know perfectly well why you want to go sailing!"

"Oh?"

"You have some harebrained notion of travelling to the Continent and trying to rescue John!"

Emma looked uncommonly guilty. Her lips parted as if to speak. He struck his fist against the wall. "Of all the unladylike, hoydenish, idiotic ideas I have ever come across, this one is the absolute limit!"

Emma was strangely silent.

"You will return to Brandford House at once!" barked the earl. "And you will put this ridiculous scheme right out of your mind!"

Emma's mouth turned down and dejection showed in every line of her being. Slowly, she rose to her feet, but still she said nothing.

If Miss Quince or Miss Foxall had been present, they could have warned the Earl of Brandford to beware. They could have told him that he had mishandled the situation, and informed him that unless he could explain to Emma, logically and coherently, why she should not undertake this venture, she would do so despite him.

But neither Miss Quince nor Miss Foxall were there. Mistakenly, Lord Brandford assumed, as he handed Emma into the carriage, that he had cowed her into submission.

IN OBEDIENCE WITH his lordship's instructions, the coachman started in the direction of Brandford House. Emma soon let him know that that was not what she had in mind.

"Billingsgate, if you please, Harry."

"Billingsgate?" questioned the coachman.

"Billingsgate!"

Harry, the coachman, was quite shocked. Billingsgate was a fish market. It was noisy, common, vulgar, rumbustious—hardly the place where a lady would venture.

Still, he consoled himself as he drove the carriage through the City's ancient, narrow, winding streets towards the Thames, ladies of fashion had their funny little ways...and who was he to argue?

EMMA HAD FORMED A PLAN. Billingsgate, she reasoned, being a fish market, was bound to have fishermen milling about. Fishermen knew about ships, and fishermen might— if suitably reimbursed—tell her of a ship that was sailing to the Continent.

It was not long before Emma caught sight of a fisherman walking up Fish Street Hill. She leaned out of the carriage window and beckoned to him.

"How would you like to earn an honest guinea?"

IT WAS AFTER MIDNIGHT when Emma slipped out of Brandford House. She carried a large sum of French francs concealed about her person. She was dressed in a coat and breeches, with her blond curls hidden under a battered felt hat.

Emma had a brace of loaded pistols in her belt, a file for sawing through barred windows was in her pocket and sev-

eral other terribly unladylike items were hidden throughout
the rest of her clothing.

Emma walked eastwards until, in Piccadilly, she saw a
hackney carriage. She hailed it and in a voice as deep as she
could make it, asked to be taken to Aldersgate Pump.

From there she would walk to the ship. She would sleep
in her cabin. At dawn, when the tide changed, she would be
sailing down the Thames and onto the high seas.

LORD BRANDFORD DISMISSED his valet. His nightshirt
looked reproachfully at him from the bed, but he made no
move to put it on. In his shirtsleeves and breeches, and no
stockings on his feet, he paced up and down the carpeted
room.

"Why am I so restless?" he asked himself irritably.

There had been nothing to vex him tonight. On the contrary, the dinner party had been perfect—or nearly perfect.
Lavinia had had a headache, which was a pity. But otherwise, the whole affair had gone splendidly.

"Why can't I sleep?" Lord Brandford glanced balefully
at the French ormolu clock on the mantelpiece. It was half
past one. "Perhaps if I lie down and close my eyes..."

He flung himself upon the bed and waited for sleep to
overcome him. When, ten seconds later, it had failed to do
so, he opened his eyes, sat up and stared ahead of him.

He had a fine view of his clothes, hanging untidily over
an Egyptian chair by the fire. He had put them there himself. His valet would never have been so careless.

The stockings transfixed him.

"Emma!" he murmured.

The entire incident at Messrs. Dapp & Hisscoke came
flooding back. *Why was I so angry with her?* he wondered.
He had almost killed her.

"And for what?" he whispered. "Because she took off a
pair of stockings?"

No, an inner voice answered him. *It wasn't that. It was because she attracted the attention of every single man in the vicinity.*

"Nonsense," he retorted. "If it had been my mother or my sister or..."

You were jealous! the inner voice told him bluntly.

Lord Brandford leapt off the bed. "I was jealous? But why? Why should I be jealous?" He prowled about the room. "There is absolutely no reason for me to be jealous of Emma. After all, it is not as though I am in love with her!"

Isn't it? the inner voice enquired.

"Of course not!" snapped Lord Brandford. "I am not in love with Emma! I can't possibly be in love in Emma! Emma drives me mad!"

He went to the fireside and gave the fire a poke. The flames danced before his eyes. He added some coal, but it was damp, and smoked. He retreated, coughing.

"Faugh! It smells just like a battlefield in here!"

Talavera. All at once, memories he had striven to suppress rose to the fore. He relived it all: the noise of the cannon, the thunder of horses' hooves. Victory in the morning, before the blazing hot July sun was too high in the sky. And then there had been the wounded, the dying; the screams of torment... and the dead.

A long shudder passed through his frame. He closed his eyes in anguish. "When you love someone and they die, you want to shut out the pain," he muttered.

And he had. For nearly three years after his father's death he had seen to it that his emotions had been locked away, so that he would not feel the agony he had felt then. Then Emma had burst into his life, sliding down the bannisters, knocking down Lady Marcella, facing him boldly, turning his whole world upside down. He had done everything he could to keep her at bay. And still she had succeeded in storming his heart.

"I am in love with Emma!" he confessed dazedly. *"I am in love with Emma!"*

And he was going to marry Lavinia.

"GOOD MORNING, LAVINIA!"

"Good morning, Charles." Lavinia Smythe received the earl in her breakfast parlour, a pleasant room which caught the morning sun. She tried to smile welcomingly at him.

"Is your headache any better?" he enquired solicitously.

Lavinia shook her head. She sat down upon a delicately carved Chippendale chair, upholstered in apricot, and indicated that he should take the one opposite.

"And it is such a shame," she observed, "since I have been receiving endless congratulations, and there is so much to be done...before our wedding."

Lord Brandford saw the opening he had been waiting for. "Lavinia..."

"Yes?"

"I have something to say to you."

"I am listening, Charles."

"Er—it's about our wedding," he began awkwardly.

"Yes, Charles?"

Lord Brandford gazed at her ingratiating expression and hated himself. "I—I beg your forgiveness, but...I cannot go through with it."

Lavinia stared at him. "I—I beg your pardon?"

"I cannot marry you, Lavinia."

Lavinia was bewildered. "I am sorry...I don't understand you.... It's this headache...."

"I cannot marry you, Lavinia," reiterated the earl. "I must ask you to release me from our engagement."

"I—I cannot have heard you aright, Charles."

"Yes, you have."

"I have? But..." Slowly, it dawned on Lavinia that he was in earnest. He really did intend to break their engagement. "Oh!" she exclaimed at length. "You have more courage than I!"

"What do you mean?"

"I knew I should never have accepted your proposal." Tears sprang to her sapphire-blue eyes. "I've been in love with John for an age. I knew he was the only man for me. But I was so angry with him, for when—when we met, he—he told me he wouldn't marry me...until the war was over."

"You were engaged?"

"N-not exactly. We—we had an understanding. He—he had a ring made for me, but I never wore it. We were not to become engaged until the fighting was over—until Bonaparte was defeated."

Lord Brandford offered her his handkerchief. She seized it gratefully and, still weeping copiously, poured them both a cup of tea.

Presently she continued. "I had waited three years, and I was becoming impatient. My friends teased me, called me an old maid. It was so important to me to prove to them..." She paused and delicately blew her nose. "Ah! How little any of that matters now!"

Lord Brandford sipped his tea in silence.

Lavinia turned her blue eyes beseechingly towards him. "I thought I had waited long enough, and I told John so. When he asked me to go on waiting, I said I wouldn't. Then you proposed...and I accepted you."

"Poor Lavinia!" murmured Lord Brandford sympathetically.

Lavinia sobbed bitterly.

"Oh, come now! Don't take it so to heart! We have both made mistakes. But they are not irretrievable! I am sure our families and our friends will understand."

"It is not that!" Lavinia managed through her tears. "It is because John has been taken prisoner. The French will kill him. And it is all my fault. He would never have accepted such a mission if I had not rejected him."

"Rejected him?"

"Yes," wept Lavinia. "John finally said he would marry me immediately—this year. And I told him I couldn't because I had already promised to marry you!"

"I would have withdrawn my suit if I had known."

Lavinia sobbed and shook her head. "I could never have asked you to. I was afraid people would call me a jilt. I was such a coward. I lacked your strength of character...and my weakness has very probably...driven John to his death!"

"Lavinia, you mustn't blame yourself!" He handed her another handkerchief.

Lavinia blew her nose once more. "I have been in absolute agony ever since Emma told me what John had written. It is so like him to think of me first. I have been a selfish beast! I am justly punished!"

"No more so than I!"

"You!" she exclaimed, startled.

"I proposed to you when I was in love with another. I denied my heart. I have been racked and tortured ever since."

A tremulous smile crossed her lips. "You are too generous, Charles. I don't deserve one who is so good to me."

"Not at all. I am in love with Emma."

Lavinia gaped at him. "Emma?"

"Yes. Emma."

"Emma Armstead?"

He nodded.

"But—you are always...fighting."

"I refused to admit it. I told myself that what I needed was the peace and tranquillity which a woman like you could give me. So while I longed for her, I—I offered for you."

"Oh!" squeaked Lavinia. She considered the matter earnestly. "It is true, Emma does not provide...tranquillity."

Lord Brandford's mouth quirked. "Ours has been a, how shall I put it, turbulent relationship."

"Tranquillity," continued Lavinia as if she had hardly heard him, "is not in Emma's nature." She reached across the table and clasped his hand. "Oh, Charles, are you sure you love her?"

Lord Brandford raised her hand to his lips. "I was never more sure of anything in my life!"

"Oh."

"Do you agree that our engagement should end?"

"Of course, I agree!" She dried her eyes, and a smile started to appear. Then a shadow crossed her face. "But the wedding...the arrangements... What are we to tell people?"

Lord Brandford looked cunning. "I believe we shall have to ask Mother dear to assist us."

Lavinia breathed a sigh of relief. "Yes, of course. Lady Brandford is sure to know how to deal with these matters." She passed her hand across her forehead.

"Is anything wrong?"

"No...nothing. It's just that my headache is gone. Strange."

"Excellent." Lord Brandford inclined his head. "Are you satisfied?"

"Completely. It is the best thing for both of us, I am sure of it." She had dried her eyes. "But please, Charles, there is one small favour I should like to ask of you."

"Name it."

"Let me go to Brandford House with you and talk to Emma." She saw him frown, and stumbled on hastily. "I— I think I can persuade her to—to give John up."

Lord Brandford hesitated. "She may be hurt. She...loves him."

Lavinia shook her head. "No. I don't believe she does."

Lord Brandford's heart leapt. He wanted to dance for joy. He had to fight to restrain himself. "I—I wish I could be so certain, but there have been...indications...."

"Oh, Charles! You are a man! You see her actions as a man does. I am a woman and my instincts—"

Lord Brandford shifted restlessly in his chair. "Her words, her manner..."

"Could have been misread."

His mouth set in a stubborn line.

"Oh, Charles!" Gently, Lavinia endeavoured to win him over. "We have *both* been blind."

"Perhaps, but Emma—"

"Is not predictable."

"What do you mean?"

Her shoulders lifted infinitesimally. "I tried to ignore it—you may have done so too—but deep down inside me, I have felt for a long time that their engagement was...a pretence."

Lord Brandford looked doubtful.

"Trust me in this matter!"

"You could be wrong." He could not entirely suppress the note of hope in his voice even as he made the suggestion.

"Even if I am wrong about Emma," countered Lavinia, "I know John. He does not love her. When he finds I am free..." There was no need to complete the sentence.

"NOT HERE?" DEMANDED the Earl of Brandford. "What do you mean Emma is not here?"

Lady Brandford adjusted her lacy parasol. She arranged herself upon a garden seat in the shade of the apple tree.

"If you had had breakfast with us like a civilized human being," she chided, "you would know."

"Know what?"

"Emma left me a letter. She apologized profusely for taking such a hurried leave of us, but said she would explain everything when she returned, which she hoped would be before your wedding. She thanked me very prettily for our hospitality."

Lord Brandford sighed exasperatedly and brushed a fallen apple blossom from his shoulder. "Where has she gone?"

Lady Brandford shrugged maddeningly. "She did not say."

Lady Marcella, stooping to admire a yellow iris, remarked, "Emma might have left a forwarding address with the servants. We merely assumed she had gone to Houghton Regina."

"She probably has." Lord Brandford picked up a silver bell and rang it.

Wooster appeared, as if by magic.

"Wooster, did Miss Armstead leave any forwarding address?"

"No, your lordship."

"At what time did she depart?"

"I have made enquiries among the staff, your lordship, and I regret to inform you that no one knows."

Lord Brandford's dark eyebrows knit across the bridge of his nose. "What do you mean?"

"Miss Armstead left without anyone's being aware of it."

Lavinia started. "But that is impossible!" she cried.

"Exactly," agreed Lady Brandford. "She cannot simply have vanished in a puff of smoke! She must have sent for a carriage...."

Wooster solemnly shook his head. "No, my lady."

A sudden cold shaft of fear shot through the earl's frame. *Last night...last night...* he thought, recalling how at dinner Lavinia had been pale and withdrawn. She had hardly uttered a word, then excused herself and departed early, saying she had a headache.

Emma, on the other hand, had been animated and lively. She had talked to everyone—even the most boring people on the guest list. Lord Brandford had been grateful to her. Her charm had gone a long way to smoothing his path with several important people. Then, all at once, he recollected something else about her manner: there had been an air of suppressed excitement. Lord Brandford's mouth felt suddenly dry.

Silently urging himself to remain calm, he asked his butler, "Wooster, would you be good enough to summon the coachman who drove Miss Armstead yesterday?"

"Certainly, my lord."

As Wooster departed, the Earl of Brandford addressed the ladies. "At what time did Emma return here yesterday morning?"

"About lunch time, was it not?" enquired Lady Brandford of her companions.

"Yes," agreed Lady Marcella, "for I told her she would have to hurry and change."

"Then she went out again afterwards," added Lavinia.

Although Lord Brandford's unease was growing by the second, he concealed it well.

Meanwhile, the coachman was brought out. He looked nervous, and his eyes darted apprehensively from Lord Brandford to the ladies.

"Harry!" announced Wooster.

Lord Brandford smiled encouragingly. "I believe you drove Miss Armstead around yesterday?"

"Yes, my lord."

"Can you tell me exactly where she went?"

"Well I, er..." Harry needed this job. He could not afford to lose it.

The earl divined what was holding him back. "It's all right, Harry," he assured the man. "You shall not be dismissed."

Harry was vastly relieved. "First we went to Messrs. Dapp & Hisscoke," he began. "Then, when you handed Miss Armstead into the carriage afterwards, we should have come here, but—" he licked his lips "—she said I was to go to Billingsgate."

Lavinia went white. "Billingsgate!"

"Yes, Miss Smythe."

Lady Brandford passed her a bottle of sal volatile.

"Please continue," requested Lord Brandford.

"Miss Armstead had me stop," proceeded Harry, "while she talked with a fisherman. Then she had me wait while she went away for a while...."

"How long?" questioned the Earl.

"About twenty minutes."

Lord Brandford frowned worriedly. "And then?"

"We went to Messrs. Grasshopper & Rice, the bankers."

"And when you finished there?" prompted his lordship.

"We came here."

"She went out again in the afternoon," stated the earl. "Where did she go?"

Harry fidgeted uneasily. "We went to a gunsmith's. I don't recall the name. Then to a rag-and-bone man—begging your pardon, your lordship—and got a suit of boys' clothes."

Lord Brandford ran his hand distractedly through his dark brown hair. "Did she go anywhere else?"

"Back to Billingsgate. Then here."

Lord Brandford clicked his tongue. His worst fears had been confirmed. "Thank you, Harry. You may go." As Harry bowed and left, the earl addressed the butler. "Wooster, would you please instruct the servants that none of this—including Miss Armstead's departure—is to be mentioned."

"Very good, my lord."

No sooner had Wooster returned to the house than Lady Marcella grasped her brother's arms. "What does it mean, Charles? What on earth is going on?"

"Yesterday, Emma asked me if I had a ship," answered Lord Brandford. "She wanted the use of it. I refused her." He swallowed. "It would seem she, er, obtained one elsewhere."

"A ship!" exclaimed Lady Brandford. "What on earth should she want a ship for?"

The light dawned upon her daughter first. "Do you mean Emma has gone to France?" demanded Lady Marcella.

"Yes," answered her brother. "Dressed as a boy."

Lavinia Smythe did the only ladylike thing possible in the circumstances: once again, and with inimitable grace, she fainted.

WHEN LADY MARCELLA returned from taking Lavinia home, Lady Brandford voiced the question uppermost in both their minds. "What are you going to do about Emma, Charles?"

"I shall go after her, of course," replied the earl.

Lady Brandford's lips quivered, and her expression was mirrored in her daughter's face. It was evident that they disapproved, and that they were anxious, but neither of them said anything. They knew from the way Lord Brandford spoke that it was useless to try to dissuade him.

CHAPTER ELEVEN

OWING TO THE CIRCUITOUS route Emma's vessel, the *Fortuna*, took, it was three days before she landed on the French coast.

Emma was not a good sailor. So, although the weather was fine and the sea was calm, she felt continually queasy. Most of the time she spent in her cabin, which was boring and none too pleasant.

It was a great relief to Emma when at last, in the early hours of the morning, she was able to disembark on a stretch of unpatrolled beach. She waded ashore, carrying her stockings and her shoes in one hand and a satchel filled with necessities in the other.

When her feet were dry, she brushed off the sand and waved to the sailors in the longboat as they rowed back to the *Fortuna*. They would continue westwards to Cherbourg and south to Aquitaine. They were seeking brandy, wine and dried fruit, offering in exchange greatcoats, bolts of wool and leather boots. It was one of the scandals of the war that the members of His Majesty's Government had cellars stocked with contraband brandy, while the Emperor's armies marched in British-made uniforms.

Emma put on her stockings and shoes. She strapped the satchel to her back, stood up and cast a glance behind her. The *Fortuna* was hoisting sail, and all at once she realized that she was alone.

For a moment, she felt a stab of fear, then resolutely gathered her courage. She was no longer seasick and she was as free as a bird. She was going to rescue Lord Druce, and though she had no regrets, she had no plans, either.

Her father had taught her never to plan, "for if you do not know the exact strength, movements and intentions of your enemy, your plans are certain to go awry." In instances where one did not have all the facts, the late Colonel Armstead had instructed, it was much better to improvise, and that was what Emma proposed to do.

Her first task was to "improvise" a route to Paris. She had no maps or charts, but she soon managed it, thanks to her father. Being a soldier, the late Colonel Armstead had impressed upon his daughter the importance of geography. When they had visited this area during the Peace of Amiens, he had taught Emma the names of the towns and villages situated on various thoroughfares leading to the capital, as well as something of the topography of the region. Now this knowledge stood her in good stead. She remembered everything and in no time she was on her way.

Delighted with her achievement, Emma walked jauntily along the road to Paris. Her progress, she reckoned, was good. Her French passed muster. She ought to have reached the capital before the end of the week.

Unfortunately, being attired in boys' clothes posed its problems. Over the years, more and more men had been pressed into the army, and the minimum age had been constantly lowered, so that conscripts were getting younger and younger.

Emma looked exactly like a reluctant, youthful conscript. She was arrested in St. Lot, in Normandy.

"Always tell the truth" her late father had advised, with the addendum "whenever possible."

Tearing open her jacket to reveal her shapely form, Emma cried, "But I am a woman!" Then she burst into tears in the presence of five embarrassed gendarmes.

Ten capacious damp linen handkerchiefs were required before she finished the incoherent tale of how she had left home, against the wishes of those who had charge of her, to see her betrothed, but Emma was eventually released.

By then she was dressed, courtesy of the mayor's wife, who had come to hear of her sad story, in women's clothes. She had a set of documents, by gracious permission of the mayor, the sole authority in St. Lot, which were a vast improvement upon the forged ones she had bought in London.

Among other things, the documents stated that she was a citizen of the Low Countries and had been born in Amsterdam. Emma had not said that: the mayor's wife had decreed it. And Emma felt it would be churlish to disappoint her.

She also had a scolding from the mayor's wife, a lecture from the mayor and a fine of fifty francs.

It's lucky I didn't have the rest of my money on me, thought Emma as she trudged on, *or my pistols, or my satchel! If I had, they would have taken me for an English spy!*

By good fortune, however, Emma had hidden these things in the hollow of a tree before she had walked into St. Lot to buy food. So, despite several factors, the chief being her age, which had set tongues wagging and resulted in her subsequent arrest, the people of St. Lot did not suspect that she was from the other side of the Channel.

True, Emma's blond hair, her blue eyes, her gestures and her non-French intonation had marked her as a foreigner. But the authorities—that is to say, the mayor, the mayor's wife and the gendarmes—being unaccustomed to British speech, had simply assumed she was Dutch. It was a verdict with which the citizenry of St. Lot would not have argued, and Emma could not have been more pleased. A sense of elation buoyed her up as she continued on her journey to Paris.

LUCK WAS WITH HER, and she reached the capital without further incident. In a matter of hours, she found herself lodgings not far from the Fontaine de l'Eléphant, a grotesque wooden structure, which marked the site of the now-demolished Bastille.

As a woman on her own, Emma aroused no comment. The French Revolution and the wars that followed had taken the lives of nearly a million Frenchmen. Many more were either fighting or being conscripted or on guard duty somewhere in Napoleon's Empire. Further thousands—from the Comte d'Artois to General Bernadotte—had emigrated.

The entire economic fabric of the country was passing into the hands of women: the wives, daughters, sisters and sweethearts who waited for their menfolk to return, and the innumerable widows, who knew they never would.

Women ran everything from the business of manufacturing cloth, to the business of making champagne. There was no question of their staying at home, for they had to seek work to earn the money their menfolk used to make.

So, the moment he clapped eyes on Emma, her landlord took it for granted that she had come to Paris to find a job.

Emma did her best to satisfy him. She applied for several jobs in the vicinity. Her interviews, always ending in failure, served two purposes. First, they lulled the landlord's suspicions; and second, they provided Emma with a reasonable explanation for the long absences which occurred when she went to reconnoitre the area around the prison where Lord Druce was confined.

The Chateau Morphise was not one of the better-known detention centres in France: it was hidden in the Forest of Vincennes, and from its appearance, had once been somebody's country estate.

Round towers, with roofs like pointed hats, marked each of its corners, and an elegant horseshoe staircase led up to the front entrance. A miniature lake, dominated by an elaborate artificial cascade, lay before the entrance, but behind a wrought-iron gate, worked with scrolls.

It is idyllic! reflected Emma, dreamily. Then she saw the sentries, who were armed.

Emma realized immediately that though the Chateau Morphise seemed pleasant enough, it had been chosen to deter would-be escapers. And even though, by this time, Lord Druce would no longer be in irons, it would be no simple task to get him out.

If they did manage to get away without being shot, mused Emma, they would run the risk of losing themselves in the forest, and might wander aimlessly without food or proper clothing, exposed to the rigours of the elements. Her father had impressed upon her how easy it was to die in such conditions.

Pensively, Emma walked around the Chateau Morphise. The walls surrounding the grounds were ten feet high, and very solid. By standing back, Emma was able to see the uppermost windows of the Chateau itself: they were barred. Emma deduced that the lower windows were the same, and that the doors were probably strongly locked and bolted.

I shall have to think of a scheme which will overcome all these obstacles, decided Emma. Meanwhile, there would be no harm in purchasing a few useful items....

EMMA SPENT THE NEXT FEW days shopping, and when she had gathered supplies to meet every contingency, she resolved to screw up her courage and go to see Lord Druce.

As yet, she had formed no idea of how he might escape, but felt that was of little consequence, since she did not intend to discuss escaping yet.

She intended merely to make contact with Lord Druce. Then, perhaps through an intermediary, they could exchange messages. He would tell her of conditions inside the Chateau; she would send him advice about the area outside.

Together we shall devise a foolproof escape plan, she thought optimistically. First, however, she had to take her supplies out of Paris, for it would be perfectly useless escaping from the Chateau Morphise only to have to return to Paris. The city was walled, like a gaol, and at the first hint of trouble—so Emma's landlord had informed her—the gates would be closed. In such a case, Paris would become an unassailable fortress to those caught outside; an impenetrable place of confinement to those caught inside. Exchanging one prison for another, Emma concluded, simply would not do.

AMONG OTHER THINGS, Emma had purchased a cart, driven by a donkey, Clytemnestra. Her former owners, Euripedes and Sophronia, had explained that Clytemnestra's companion, Solon, had died. "She loved poor Solon passionately. Now that he is gone, she is sure to die of grief. She needs another companion, but alas, we cannot afford to buy her one. So we must either break our hearts watching her pine away, or sell her."

Emma only half believed their story. But she could not resist Clytemnestra, with her soft grey ears and her sad brown eyes.

The Greeks knew it. Mentally they calculated how much money they would be able to wring from Emma for the animal. They did not ask her why she wanted Clytemnestra, for like the captain and the crew of the *Fortuna,* they suspected that Emma's purpose was something they would rather not know, though they decided they could charge extra, in return for being discreet. But they were in an even better position than the captain and the crew of the *Fortuna*—for though there were several ships available to Emma, there was only one donkey—and the Greeks, in the end, were able to exact quite a stiff price for Clytemnestra.

TIME IS OF THE ESSENCE! Emma told herself.

Assuming that Lord Brandford and Lavinia had not cancelled their wedding, she had until Saturday, May 30. Twelve days had passed since she had left London, and another day had been lost before that while she had planned her departure. She had almost two and a half weeks, she calculated, to rescue John from the Chateau Morphise and to get him back to England.

That was her top limit. It afforded her an ample sufficiency of days and nights to accomplish her task. However, her late father had warned her never to ignore the unexpected. "Accidents can happen. Unlooked-for delays can occur. It is never wise to be too optimistic in these cases."

No, indeed, agreed Emma. It would not do if they arrived at the church while the wedding was actually in progress. Lavinia would hardly thank her for that! And as for Lord Brandford—his reaction to such an event was not to be contemplated!

Thus it was that Emma reached her decision to combine the hiding of the supplies with a visit to Lord Druce.

EMMA LOADED EVERYTHING into the cart, harnessed Clytemnestra to it, and led her through the city gates into the Forest of Vincennes.

Clytemnestra was an obedient animal. She showed no resistance when Emma tied her up by a tree and told her to wait. After she had talked to John, Emma resolved that she would find somewhere safe in the woods to store everything.

THE SUN WAS SHINING through the trees and a gentle breeze was blowing when Emma walked up to the gates of the Chateau Morphise and announced that she had come to visit one of the prisoners: an Englishman, Monsieur Druce.

The gendarmes demanded to see her papers, and Emma thrust them through the scrolled ironwork.

The gendarmes opened the gates and let Emma in. When she had advanced a few steps, more gendarmes appeared. They, too, demanded to see her papers, and Emma obliged them.

"Do you have permission from the Governor to see Monsieur Druce?"

"No," answered Emma truthfully.

The gendarmes grunted and told her to proceed to the cascade, where another squad of gendarmes approached. They scrutinized her papers as well, then shook their heads.

"We must inform the Governor."

Emma trembled.

What if the Governor decides to have me searched? she wondered. The late Colonel Armstead had warned her that searches in French prisons were *very* thorough. *Mercy me!* lamented Emma inwardly.

Luck was with her, however. The Governor had an aviary in a secluded part of the gardens of the Chateau Morphise. To his collection of grey nuthatches, yellow wagtails and blue rock thrushes, he had just added a pair of rosefinches brought from the far-distant Caucasus.

These rosefinches were infinitely more absorbing to the Governor than Emma, and he did not trouble to examine her, or to have her searched, but simply sent down word that she might go through with her visit.

Emma was taken to the rear of the Chateau. There, on the lawn, groups of prisoners were talking, gambling or smoking.

She saw Lord Druce at once: he was scraping the ashes out of a clay pipe. As she drew near him, he glanced up. His face registered surprise, shock, consternation and horror.

"What are you doing here?" he gasped.

Emma smiled seraphically at him. Until then, she had intended to frame her sentences carefully; to play an elaborate game of hide-and-seek; to resort to a sort of verbal subterfuge.

Now she saw that the strain would be too much for Lord Druce; her visit alone had unnerved him. What would the tension and secrecy of a long-planned escape do to his mind? He had to be protected from such a catastrophe. But how?

All at once, Emma seemed to hear Colonel Armstead's voice. "Be bold!" he exhorted. "Catch the enemy off guard! Strike when he least expects it, and you cannot fail to conquer!"

Emma took her beloved parent at his word. "I have come," she announced, "to help you escape."

Lord Druce looked as if he were going to collapse. "No!" he croaked. "That's impossible!"

His hazel eyes flickered in the direction of the gendarmes, who were lounging about not more than ten feet away.

They had been engaged in supervising half a dozen prisoners whose duty it was to clean the windows upon the ground floor, where the Governor had his offices.

It was fatiguing work, watching the prisoners, which is why the gendarmes were now sitting down with their feet up and their hats over their eyes.

"Have you given your word that you wouldn't?" enquired Emma.

"Of course not!"

"Then there is nothing to keep you here."

Lord Druce made a choking sound. He stared fixedly a the gendarmes' rifles.

"You must escape," continued Emma blithely, "be cause otherwise Lavinia is going to marry Charles, and they will be absolutely miserable together."

Lord Druce dragged his gaze back to Emma. She had no troubled to lower her voice, and several of the other pris oners had heard her. Fascinated, they had stopped what ever they were doing. Now they were hanging on her every word, drawing closer in order not to miss anything.

"This is a joke, isn't it, Emma?" Lord Druce nodded his head vigorously, indicating what answer she ought to give.

Emma shook her head in negation. "No, it isn't."

"It *is* a joke!" insisted Lord Druce. "It *is* a joke!" He uttered a hollow laugh and eyed his fellow captives plead ingly, his look begging them to go away. But they were far too engrossed in the conversation to take the hint.

"I am quite serious," Emma assured him. "The only question is, how? Now, since you know the inside of the Chateau and I know the outside, I thought that perhaps you could break out—tonight possibly—and climb over the wall. Then I would meet you with some fast horses, and—"

"Emma," interrupted Lord Druce wearily. "It is fool hardy even to attempt to escape from the Chateau Mor phise. Do you see those cannons?"

Emma glanced up at the roof. There were five cannons placed at intervals below the dormer windows, where the servants' quarters had once been.

"Two nights ago," proceeded Lord Druce, "Ivor Jones tried to escape, and those cannons were fired at him. He came back. If he had not, he would have been blown to bits."

Emma shuddered.

"He is in irons. They are going to send him to the gal leys."

Emma grimaced, then she brightened. "Couldn't we take him with us when we go?"

Lord Druce closed his hazel eyes as if he were in pain.

By now the gendarmes had come to investigate the knot of prisoners crowded round Emma and Lord Druce. They pushed their way through, demanding to know what was going on.

The gendarmes did not seem to have a sense of humour, for the mention of escape plans did not make them laugh, and they were not one little bit amused to hear that Emma was talking—as bold as brass—of rescuing Ivor Jones, the man in irons.

They were also ill-bred: as soon as they knew what was going on, they began to rant and rave, and their language was most unseemly.

"There is no need to shout!" Emma rebuked them. "It is perfectly ridiculous of you not to expect people to discuss escaping. Nobody should be in this prison in the first place—" She paused at the sound of a loud cheer from the men. "After all, what have they done? They were only fighting for their country. And some weren't even doing that, they were merely travelling across Europe—"

"Mademoiselle," interrupted the senior gendarme, "the Emperor has decreed ..."

"Bah! The Emperor! He is utterly in the wrong, and he knows it!"

"Treason! Treason!" shouted the gendarmes.

Lord Druce put his head in his hands.

The gendarmes were livid. They declared they would not stand by and hear the Emperor insulted. One of them seized Emma, and another took hold of Lord Druce, as two more, convinced they were about to expose an elaborate plot, hurried to fetch Ivor Jones for a confrontation.

"What do you think you are doing?" Emma's tones would have done credit to Miss Foxall and Miss Quince at their most affronted.

"You are under arrest!" screamed the gendarme furiously.

Emma, her head held high, prepared to submit. She marched alongside the gendarme in the direction of the main building. Unfortunately, because she was looking up, she did not see the bucket, which one of the prisoners, who had been cleaning the windows, had placed right in her path.

Emma tripped, and lost her balance. The gendarme holding on to her tried to steady her, but lost his balance, vainly endeavoring to steady himself. His foot splashed in the soapy water, as his other foot interlocked with Emma's leg, and down they went onto the green grass together, amid hoots of laughter from the bored prisoners.

The gendarme holding Lord Druce, his face red with anger, came over to help his comrade, just as a prisoner, more mischievous than his companions, extended a broom handle. The gendarme fell on top of his colleague, hitting his head on the bucket, which knocked him out.

Meanwhile, the other gendarmes had returned with the luckless Ivor Jones, still in irons. Dropping him, they charged into the fray, crying, "Surrender!" interspersed with other less-polite expressions.

But by now, everything was out of their hands. They were struck from behind and rendered unconscious. At once, the prisoners seized their rifles and their keys, and Ivor Jones was released from his irons. Together with Emma and Lord Druce, he was propelled towards the wall.

As Lord Druce had said, the cannon had been fired, but in the dark, the cannoneers had aimed too low, and the top of the wall had been demolished. In two or three places, it was no longer ten feet high; it was merely eight feet high.

The prisoners did not even need ropes, but stood on one another's shoulders. They clambered onto the crumbling fortifications, hauling their companions up after them. By the time they descended, Emma's clean white cotton dress was quite, quite ruined.

If Miss Quince and Miss Foxall could see me now! she thought, as her feet touched terra firma.

It was over so quickly. By the time the other gendarmes realized what had happened and were ready to fire their cannon, it was too late, and some thirty-odd prisoners were running free in the Forest of Vincennes.

EMMA CAUGHT HOLD of Lord Druce and dragged him to the cart.

Lord Druce stared as if struck with horror as she untied Clytemnestra. "You're not going to suggest that we escape in *that*!"

"Of course not! This poor old jenny won't take us very far. But I have clothing and other provisions."

At least nineteen of the prisoners pricked up their ears. If they changed clothes, if they had wigs or scarves or hats, strong stout shoes or boots, they had a better chance of success.

LORD DRUCE WORE A MARTYRED expression as he and the rest of the men changed behind some rather impish bushes which kept poking them in the most undesirable places.

Emma attired herself inside the cart itself, hidden from view by a large canvas. She emerged looking like a Normandy peasant girl, in a rough woollen dress with a white linen cap and wooden clogs.

By now the alarm had been given. The gendarmes were issuing forth from the Chateau Morphise, their shouts of rage echoing throughout the forest. The escaped prisoners were anxious to be off—but where? The light was fading, and the forest was growing dark.

Some cried one thing and some cried another, but it was Emma who settled it. To Lord Druce's amusement, she declared that she had taken note of the various routes, and she knew how to guide them out.

Behind them they could hear the pursing gendarmes, their lanterns flickering through the trees. They could hear shots as the gendarmes fired at shadows. But the darkness of the night, the quietness of their exit and the trees themselves gave Emma and her party all the cover they needed.

OF THE ORIGINAL GROUP, fifteen prisoners had already broken away. Now that they were out of the forest, the nineteen with Emma were divided once more. Nine prisoners had decided to go south. The other ten, including Lord Druce and Ivor Jones, turned north. Emma was with the latter group.

They travelled the whole night. Clytemnestra, faithful, obedient and slow, trotted along with them. The journey was an uneventful one and as dawn broke, they found themselves approaching another wood, the Forest of Senlis. Once more they were to be hidden by friendly trees.

AT THE CHATEAU MORPHISE, the dawn broke on a less than promising day for the guards. Their easygoing Governor had been dismissed, and a new one, Governor Ollivier, had been appointed.

At first, Governor Ollivier had been elated by his new command, but upon learning that more than thirty prisoners were missing, he was not pleased. Grimly, he listened to the gendarmes' explanations, deciding that his predecessor had been too lax.

"Security must be tightened!" he declared. "Now these prisoners who escaped—they had given their *parole*?"

"No, Governor," came the response.

"No? They were not asked to give their *parole* before they went into the gardens? But they were British! It is well known that the best way of keeping British prisoners secure is to require them to give their word not to escape! They always keep their word, once they give it! Why did no one take this precaution?"

There was no answer.

"In future, no prisoner will be allowed into the gardens to exercise unless he gives his word of honour not to escape! Is that clear?"

"Yes, Governor."

There followed some scathing comments about the gendarmes' shooting ability, their sloppiness and the way they had neglected to repair the wall. At length, however, a gleam lit Governor Ollivier's black eyes when one of the gendarmes told him that some discarded clothing, belonging to the prisoners, had been discovered.

"Aha!" Governor Ollivier remarked softly. "Someone has played into our hands!"

Old clothes merchants were known to the police. They could be interrogated. The items they had sold could be checked. New descriptions of the escaped prisoners could then be issued. *Le Moniteur* would help, no doubt.

"Within thirty days," vowed Colonel Ollivier, "these prisoners shall be returned to the Chateau Morphise—dead or alive!"

CHAPTER TWELVE

THE EARL OF BRANDFORD'S graceful yacht, the *Venus*, had deposited him on a deserted stretch of sandy beach between Le Havre and Dieppe. The voyage had not taken long, barely time for him to snatch forty winks.

Lord Brandford had walked from the seashore to Rouen. On the way, he had brooded about Emma, finally concluding that she would likely go to Paris, since that was the nearest city in the vicinity of the Chateau Morphise, where Lord Druce was confined.

But he could not help worrying whether she had reached Paris safely. He assumed she had, but he was not certain—and the uncertainty was driving him mad.

All right, he had told himself at length, *Emma is in Paris. She must be.* Good. That was settled.

But how was she getting on in Paris, and what was she doing? He had no doubt that she was getting into a scrape, for she was bound to get into a scrape!

Why couldn't she have waited for me? he asked bitterly. *If she had waited, I would have been there to rescue her....* But Emma never waited: she acted, and he ought to have known that, so he had gritted his teeth and walked on.

Thank heavens, Mother dear was looking after the cancellation of his and Lavinia's wedding, and in such a way that there would be no scandal—some surprise, perhaps, some consternation, even, but no scandal.

He had tried to imagine how Lady Brandford was managing in his absence—and Lady Marcella, and Lavinia, but he had been unable to keep his mind on them.

How was he to persuade Emma to come back without John? What was he to say to her when they met?

How can I explain to her that I love her, that I have loved her from the first moment I saw her, though I didn't realize it? he asked himself. And how was he going to find her so that he could tell her these things?

By the time Lord Brandford had reached Rouen in the early hours of the morning, he was tired, hungry, disgruntled and morose. He was also so scruffy that no one who had known him in London would have recognized him. His hair was unkempt, and he wore no cravat, merely a wrinkled, patched cotton shirt, partly concealed by a threadbare brown cloth waistcoat, which was old-fashioned and too large, so that it hung loosely about him.

He had chosen the Café Pierre Corneille because, apart from the delicious aroma of food and coffee issuing from its kitchens, it offered *Le Moniteur* to its customers. *Le Moniteur* was the official version of news in France, and Lord Brandford wanted, above all else, to find out what the official mind was thinking that morning. It was brought to him, along with a cup of coffee, while he waited for his breakfast.

At once his eye fell upon an account of the mass escape from the Chateau Morphise. According to Governor Ollivier, the prisoners had acted swiftly, led by a veritable Amazon. She was, Governor Ollivier surmised, an acrobat or a circus performer. She had skillfully brought down a number of his men with a well-rehearsed, theatrical tour de force....

Lord Brandford's brown eyes darkened, and he put his coffee cup clumsily down. The saucer rattled and some of the hot liquid spilled.

Emma!

He groaned. He had no objection to Lord Druce or any of the other prisoners at the Chateau Morphise escaping—far from it—but that Emma should be involved! "Acrobat, indeed!" he snorted.

It was obvious to the earl what had happened. Emma had tripped; a guard, or perhaps two guards, had gone down with her, and the prisoners had seized the chance to make a break for it.

"'Well-rehearsed theatrical tour de force,' my foot!" he concluded, glowering at *Le Moniteur,* and wondering what to do next.

His original idea to go to Paris, to make contact with Emma and to persuade her to return to England with him was no longer feasible. The escape from the Chateau Morphise had put paid to it. And now Emma had got into trouble, just as he'd known she would.

But what on earth was he to do now? he asked himself again. Just then, his breakfast arrived, briefly distracting him. Freshly baked crusty rolls, each with a generous pat of butter, another cup of coffee and a hard-boiled egg. Ravenously, he dug in.

If he only knew where they were, he could meet them, Lord Brandford reflected, but he had no idea where Emma and the others were; he did not even know whether they were still at liberty.

I shall have to wait! Lord Brandford told himself with an exasperated sigh. *I shall have to wait for further news.*

LORD BRANDFORD LEFT the Café Pierre Corneille, slouching with his head down and his hands in his pockets. He had no lodgings in Rouen, for he had not intended to stay. Now, however, he had no choice. He trudged along the cobbled streets until at last he found a place which suited him. It was plain, clean—and had more than one exit…in case of need.

He thought constantly about Emma and the thirty-odd prisoners she had inadvertently helped to escape from the Chateau Morphise. Had they broken up into smaller groups? Would they make for the coast, or would they try to go east, or perhaps south? *Le Moniteur* did not mention the fact, but Wellington's army was pushing across Spain. Would they head there? They could be anywhere! mused Lord Brandford. Finding them would be like finding a needle in a haystack!

As he sank deeper and deeper into his gloomy reverie, he glowered at anyone who spoke to him. His questions were short and brusque; his answers to others' came in mono-syllables and grunts.

The townspeople assumed he was a surly old soldier! He was limping, so obviously he had been wounded, and equally obviously, therefore, he had been in the army.

Lord Brandford knew nothing of their deductions. He was indeed limping, and his limp grew more pronounced as the day passed. But it was not an affectation, it was caused by the shoes he had purchased, which were too tight, and badly made. A small lump at the heel rubbed on Lord Brandford's foot as the day progressed. He developed a large, uncomfortable blister, which naturally was yet an-other source of irritation to him.

THE FOLLOWING MORNING, Lord Brandford returned to the Café Pierre Corneille. This time he had a pot of coffee and a roll and butter for breakfast. Again, he read *Le Moniteur*.

Governor Ollivier was crowing with triumph, for eight prisoners had already been recaptured. Furthermore, the evidence gathered showed that the prisoners had split into three groups. Governor Ollivier interpreted this as a sign of weakness: undoubtedly, they had quarrelled among them-selves.

One group, surmised Governor Ollivier, had gone north; another had gone south; the third, from which the prisoners had been captured, had attempted to go east. Governor Ollivier added that the five who were still at large from this last group would soon be back in custody.

There followed a description of the clothes which the remaining escaped prisoners were wearing. This information had been assiduously collected by Governor Ollivier, in conjunction with the Paris Police, and it had been supplied mainly by the old clothes merchants in the capital.

Lord Brandford sighed wearily as he read the article. The passage in which Governor Ollivier remarked that the escape, though well-planned, was bound to fail because of the obvious bickering among the escapers, had the earl ready to tear his hair. "Well-planned?" he snorted. It could not have been more ill-conceived!

Then Lord Brandford came to the lines which made him sit bolt upright. "'The Amazon who engineered this audacious and bloodthirsty escape,'" continued Governor Ollivier, "'is said to be with the group who have gone north. And I—I myself and none other—shall take her!'"

The earl's heart took a leap. *North!* he thought joyfully. Emma had gone north! Mentally, he listed the various ports from whence she might take a ship to England. Then fear tightened around his heart like a vice as he realized he was doing just what Ollivier was doing. Thus, the closer he came to finding Emma, the closer Ollivier would come to finding her... and the greater her danger.

I must get to Emma first! he decided. *I must find her before Ollivier does! I must be cleverer than he is. Now, where on earth would Emma go?*

GOVERNOR OLLIVIER DID NOT yet know about the donkey and the cart, nor did the prisoners he had captured so far.

Therefore, Governor Ollivier's descriptions to *Le Moniteur* were unintentionally misleading.

The good people of northern France were looking for a number of men on foot, accompanied by a fair-haired woman, but what they actually saw was Clytemnestra pulling a cart led by one man, with another man sitting up front and five, or occasionally six, men walking behind. What they did *not* see was Emma and the rest lying under canvas.

Whenever it was convenient, the escaped prisoners changed places, so that they each had a turn in the cart. Emma did her share of walking, but she did not wear women's clothes, at least, not once they left the Forest of Senlis. She dressed like a boy, with a brown wig covering her blond curls.

"THE FRENCH WILL HAVE all the ports watched," reckoned Lord Druce. "We'll have to try for a ship outside the country."

"But we can't go too far," protested Emma. "Poor Clytemnestra will never manage it."

"We'll have to shoot her, then," stated Viscount Zellinge.

He was not over-fond of Clytemnestra, because of the comfits. Emma had made a few comfits while she was still in Paris, having been told by her Greek owners that Clytemnestra had a veritable passion for comfits. So, it turned out, had Viscount Zellinge, but Clytemnestra won, and Viscount Zellinge had not forgiven her for it.

"We shall not!" retorted Emma coldly.

"Useless animal!"

"We must try our luck in Belgium," said Lord Druce quickly, hoping to avert a quarrel. "It's not very far, and we may be able to find a ship to take us home from there."

CHAPTER THIRTEEN

GOVERNOR OLLIVIER WAS baffled and angry. What had happened to the group of escaped prisoners who had gone north? They had not, surely, vanished into thin air! Yet, despite the detailed descriptions of their clothing and of the woman with them, not a single report had been received concerning them.

That she, the ringleader of this conspiracy, should slip through his fingers infuriated Governor Ollivier, and his temper rose by the hour. His subordinates noticed and kept well out of his way.

Then came the chance Governor Ollivier had been waiting for: four of the escaped prisoners who had been on their way south were recaptured, and by interrogation, Governor Ollivier learned about the donkey and the cart. For the first time in days, a smile illuminated his thin, dark features.

"Of course! No wonder they eluded us! They have transport!" he cried, so pleased that he did not scold anyone for not having ferreted out this fact before. After all, he reasoned, there had been no tracks to inform them. A heavy but short shower had seen to that. And it had been so unexpected—a donkey, of all things!

"A slow donkey and a two-wheeled cart! We must get full particulars!" Assuredly, they would not be long in coming, once the Paris Police began investigating, and then the locals would have to be asked again for their help, via *Le*

Moniteur. News of the escaped prisoners, reckoned Governor Ollivier, would come pouring in.

Twelve prisoners in custody! And another twenty-two almost within his grasp! Governor Ollivier was a happy man that night.

LORD BRANDFORD SOON decided that Emma and her companions would not be making for any port in France, given the certainty the entire French coastline would be watched—and not only because of Emma and her party.

Lord Brandford was aware that Napoleon's Continental System was in full force. British manufacturing was suffering as a result, and so was European trade. No concessions were made. All beaches and ports were regularly patrolled—at any rate, they were supposed to be. But opposition to Napoleon's Continental System was widespread, however, and smuggling was rife. Lord Brandford had heard rumours that the Russians were pulling out altogether.

All the same, he reminded himself, *I am a foreigner and an enemy here. I must take precautions.*

He laid his plans with care, paying for his rooms in Rouen, and taking a diligence to Calais. His fellow passengers were not interested in Napoleon's Continental System, but talked about nothing except the great escape from the Chateau Morphise.

In their opinion, Governor Ollivier was right, and the whole affair was a master plot. Lord Brandford's tentative suggestion that it was totally unplanned was received with hoots of derisive laughter.

"What will happen to the prisoners once they are recaptured?" enquired Lord Brandford at one point.

"Governor Ollivier declares they will go to the galleys," a wheezing fat man informed him.

"All except the woman," added a prim Normandy housewife. "She is the leader. They will guillotine her."

A shiver ran down Lord Brandford's spine.

"Bah! Nonsense!" countered an elderly schoolmaster sitting next to the earl. "They will be threatened with the galleys, certainly. But Napolean—our beloved Emperor—will spare them."

"You sound very certain," remarked Lord Brandford doubtfully.

"Of course." The schoolmaster was only too pleased to explain. "The Emperor needs men, live men, to fight for him. He is gathering another Grande Armée. He needs recruits. The escaped prisoners will be offered a choice: the galleys . . . or a French uniform."

The other passengers in the diligence declared that the escaped prisoners would be fools not to choose the latter.

"But the woman," persisted Lord Brandford, "she can't go into the army!"

The other passengers were unanimous in asserting that she would, without doubt, face the guillotine.

The earl's blood ran cold.

CAREFULLY, USING EVERY ounce of skill that he possessed, Lord Brandford followed Emma's trail.

He was absolutely certain that she and the escaped prisoners from the Chateau Morphise could not enter any of the towns, where descriptions of them would have been posted. They would have been recognized, arrested and handed over to Governor Ollivier.

They could not go to any fishing villages, especially not those with good natural harbours, for such places were regularly patrolled and well guarded.

On the other hand, they could not stay out in the open. They were too vulnerable. Not only were they exposed to the

elements, but they could be seen by any peasant and re-
ported, in which case their fate would be sealed.

Therefore, if they chose some shelter—as they had to do,
because although the days in May were balmy, the nights
were decidedly chilly—they would have to choose one which
was far away from human habitation. This alone would
make them safe from the unwanted attentions of the gen-
darmerie and possible recapture.

After leaving Calais, Lord Brandford walked all through
the day and into the night. The sandy beach before him had
no harbour, nor was it near a town. There was only one
landmark. He could see it by the light of the moon: a folly,
constructed by an eccentric nobleman, some three hundred
years earlier.

It was known locally, from its shape, as the Hexagon.
Desolate and isolated, it stood with its back to the North Sea
and its face to the sand dunes. Its roof had long been in dis-
repair. Its stone walls were beginning to crumble.

"That's it!"

Lord Brandford knew the moment he saw it that this was
where Emma and the escaped prisoners would take refuge,
not solely because it complied with the conditions he had
gone through in his mind. Before he had left England, he
had obtained permission to study some of Lord Druce's
papers, and on one of Lord Druce's own maps, various
abandoned buildings had been indicated as probable hide-
aways.

The Hexagon had been marked as the best refuge in Belgium. Lord Druce had given it his highest sign of approval.
Three neat little stars, drawn with red ink.

Lord Brandford's heart leaped. "I've found them!" he
whispered joyfully.

He did not go directly to the Hexagon, however. Instead,
he walked down to the water's edge. There was a sailor

mending his net and cursing, for he had caught no fish that day.

"Would you like to earn some money?" asked Lord Brandford.

The sailor looked suspiciously at him. "Perhaps."

"You could earn money in England."

The man laughed harshly and without humour. "You are a government official?" he asked, obviously suspecting his loyalty to Napoleon's regime was being tested.

It was the earl's turn to laugh. "Hardly." He paused. "It's a fine night. You could cross the Channel on a night like this."

"Maybe. It could be a quick journey if there is no storm."

"I could pay you to take someone to England." He felt around amongst his loose change, and offered half of what he actually had. "Twenty-five gold pieces."

The man shook his head.

"If it isn't money you want, perhaps something else will do?"

With a frosty smile, the man replied, "The only thing I want is my brother. He is a prisoner in England, in what they call the hulks."

"Ah!" breathed Lord Brandford. "I think I can help you secure his release. But you must take someone to England for me."

The man snorted. "It is too dangerous."

"I am prepared to pay," Lord Brandford reminded him. "Twenty-five gold pieces."

His nostrils flared. "My brother may not be released. And then what? I have had my trouble for nothing. I may be taken prisoner and shut up for goodness knows how long, my business may fail. I must have some security against that."

"How much do you want?"

"Fifty gold pieces."

"Done."

They shook hands.

"Do you see that building over there?" enquired Lord Brandford.

"The Hexagon? Yes. I see it."

"Be at the water's edge below it at midnight. Your passenger will wade out to meet you. I will come also to give you the money."

"Agreed."

Again they shook hands and departed.

AS HE SMILED ACROSS TO the Hexagon, Lord Brandford watched the sand dunes. There was no sign of anyone lurking, no gendarmes hiding in the sparse grass. The coastline was as barren and as deserted as the world before the creation of Man.

INSIDE THE HEXAGON, a loud knocking reverberated. The group of escaped prisoners stiffened and, seizing their rifles, aimed them at the heavy oak door.

"Who is it?" called Lord Druce.

"Charles," came the Earl of Brandford's voice. "Let me in, John."

"Are you alone?"

Lord Brandford sighed. He was tempted to reply that he had the entire French army with him, but decided against it.

"Of course."

The bolt was withdrawn from the door.

Lord Druce sprang forward to embrace the earl. "Charles, by all that is wonderful! What on earth brings you here? How did you find us?"

Lord Brandford strode into the dimly lit room, his brown eyes sweeping over the other nine men, standing or sitting on decrepit pieces of furniture.

They met his gaze warily, their firearms at the ready, their stance tense as if they were poised for an attack.

Lord Brandford hardly noticed their lack of cordiality, for he was looking for Emma. She was a little distance away from the men. Like them, she was attired scruffily in French peasants' clothing. Yet, in the candlelight, she was even more enticing than Lord Brandford had remembered.

He wanted to speak to her, to coax her to come to him, but his heart was too full. A lump rose in his throat and he could not utter a sound. Abruptly, he recollected that Lord Druce was waiting for an answer. He found his voice.

"Won't you introduce me to your friends, John?" he asked.

IT WAS ONLY NATURAL that Lord Druce should begin with Emma. "Of course," he said awkwardly, "you two know each other."

Emma curtsied automatically.

How cold he is! she reflected, her mouth curving down. *What did you expect?* a little voice inside her asked. *That he would seize you in his arms and cover you with kisses?* Emma grimaced and shuffled her foot uncertainly.

"Er, how is Lady Brandford? And Marcella?"

"They are both well. I thank you."

"And Lavinia?"

Lord Brandford shrugged negligently. "She is well, too, I imagine."

"And looking forward to your wedding?"

"Our wedding has been cancelled."

Emma felt exactly the same way she had when she had once accidently walked into the lamp-post by the Church of St. Ethelburga the Virgin, in Houghton Regina: winded and dazed.

"C-cancelled?" she stammered.

Lord Druce's mouth was hanging open.

"Lavinia and I decided that it would be best if we did not marry," said Lord Brandford.

Lord Druce looked as if he wanted to leap up and down with joy, but masterfully, he restrained himself. "Indeed?" was all he could manage.

"I daresay you will hear the whole story once we get back to England," remarked the earl.

"Er, yes—quite." Lord Druce pulled himself together and went on with the other introductions.

Meanwhile, Emma stared at Lord Brandford.

The wedding is cancelled! she thought, stunned. That meant Lavinia could marry John.... But why? Why had the wedding been cancelled? It did not make sense—unless, of course, Lavinia had admitted her love for John and asked Charles to set her free. But then, in Emma's estimation, Lavinia was hardly the kind of woman who would jilt a man, so Charles must have asked Lavinia to set him free.

But for what reason? The Earl of Brandford was hardly the kind of man who would jilt a woman. Emma was extremely perplexed.

"Charles, why—" The question was on the tip of her tongue, when she suddenly remembered there were ten other men in the room.

Botheration! she thought, making a face, *I am going to have to wait for a suitable moment.*

In the interim, the introductions having been made, Lord Druce repeated his question, "How did you find us?"

CHAPTER FOURTEEN

"I WAS GREATLY ASSISTED by Governor Ollivier," replied Lord Brandford.

"What!" exclaimed Lord Druce. "You—you have not betrayed us?"

"Not I! Dear Governor Ollivier has been publishing reports about you. Here!" He offered them the various copies of *Le Moniteur* which he had carried with him from Rouen.

They stood in little groups, reading them eagerly by the light of the candles, and exclaiming as their peril was revealed.

"That wasn't the only thing," continued Lord Brandford. "I hope you'll forgive me for this, John, but . . . I obtained permission to look through some of your papers. I found a map with certain places marked, and the Hexagon was among them."

"That's, er, perfectly all right," said Lord Druce awkwardly.

There was a brief silence while they waited for everyone to finish with *Le Moniteur*.

"But as you can see," continued Lord Brandford, "if I am able to find you, Governor Ollivier will be able to do so, as well."

Lord Druce bit his lip. "You're right! We must get out of here—quickly!"

"I think," remarked Viscount Zellinge, "the time has come for us to split up."

There was a murmur of protest from the others.

"I quite agree," said Lord Brandford smoothly. "One of the factors that enables Governor Ollivier to identify you is the size of your group."

A couple of coughs and half a dozen grunts came in response.

"I've taken steps to help you. I've found a skiff that will take one of you back to England."

"Emma should be the one to go," stated Lord Druce.

"No!" cried Emma. "It would be cowardly for me to leave everyone!'

"Not at all," replied Lord Druce. "You are a woman, and—"

"That has nothing to do with it! I have shared your danger so far—"

"Contributed to it, you mean!" interposed Lord Zellinge.

Emma flinched as if she had been struck.

Ivor Jones sprang to her defence. "If it hadn't been for her, none of us would have got out of the Chateau Morphise. You ought to remember that, Zellinge."

"*Lord* Zellinge, if you please, *Mr.* Jones." The Viscount waved *Le Moniteur* at Emma. "Governor Ollivier has only to publish your description and we're sunk. That is why *you* must go back to England on that boat. You're a danger to us all. You—"

"That will do!" interrupted Lord Brandford coldly.

Emma, close to tears, spun on her heel and made for an inner door.

Lord Zellinge opened his mouth to speak again.

The expression on Lord Brandford's face made him shut it with a snap.

"I should like to speak to Miss Armstead *alone*," said the earl.

Then, before anyone had a chance to object, he seized one of the candles and followed Emma out.

EMMA HAD GONE THROUGH the maze of rooms as far from the others as she could. She put her candle down and was trying to dry her eyes when Lord Brandford appeared.

As he placed his candle beside hers on an empty, up-turned barrel, Emma braced herself for a dry, humourless professorial lecture, certain that he would deliver a sermon of the kind one receives from an irate, unsympathetic clergyman.

Emma was too overwrought to submit tamely to this type of reprimand. She had been deeply hurt by Lord Zellinge's unkind cuts and if the Earl of Brandford added any more sharp rejoinders of his own, she was ready to lash out at him, to wound him as cruelly as Lord Zellinge had wounded her.

But Lord Brandford did not speak. Instead, he cupped her face in his hands with a tenderness that took her breath away.

"Emma..." His tone was soft and caressing. "I—I love you."

Emma gave a tiny gasp. Hope and disbelief warred within her as his lips brushed hers with a delicacy of touch she had not thought he possessed.

"I have loved you since the moment I first saw you. When you slid down the bannisters at the Houghton Academy for Young Ladies, you slid straight into my heart."

Emma's eyes were wide with amazement. "B-but...you...you were so angry..."

"I know. I'm sorry. Forgive me."

Emma's resistance crumbled. "Charles..." She reached out to him.

Lord Brandford drew her towards him, allowing her to cling to his manly form. "I didn't understand myself...

hen. I—I wanted to crush you to me, to smother you with my kisses. I—I wanted to pour my love over you…like a libation."

Emma buried her face in his chest. Tears of joy were trickling down her cheeks.

"I wish I had," he said. "I—I tried to deny my heart. I…my father…my father's death still affected me. I didn't want to feel…to love someone only to have them torn from me. The agony would have been unendurable."

Emma's arms tightened around him.

"That's why I tried to make myself marry Lavinia. I thought it would be better if I had someone who did not…move me as you did. I thought I should be safe from hurt. I…used her in a desperate attempt to lock my feelings away…."

Emma dabbed her eyes.

"It was like lying on a bed of nails!"

Her fingers played with his lapels.

"Finally I could stand it no longer—"

"So that is why…you are not going to marry Lavinia."

"That's right. I couldn't. I love you too much."

"Oh!" Emma murmured blissfully.

Instinctively, she tilted her face up to be kissed, in a gesture he could not resist.

"Is Lavinia very upset?" murmured Emma after a while.

"No. I thought she would be, but…it seems she is in love…with John."

"Yes." Emma's voice was scarcely above a whisper. "I know."

"You know?" He was surprised.

"I have known for some time."

There was a catch in her voice, which Lord Brandford misunderstood. Despite the way she had melted at his touch, he was convinced that she was distressed by the discovery of

Lavinia's love for Lord Druce. To spare her, he spoke o
other things.

"That's why I hired the skiff," he stated. "I must get yo
away from here, Emma. You must agree to go."

Her glance was half enquiring, half defiant. "Must?"

"It is essential."

"Why?"

"Governor Ollivier intends to make you the scapegoat fo
the incompetence of the gendarmes at the Chateau Mor
phise. You are in greater danger than the rest."

"Really? They could be shot," countered Emma, "or sen
to the galleys."

"Not according to the French people on the diligence
took from Rouen to Calais. They believe the men will b
offered the opportunity to fight in the French army."

"Hah!" snorted Emma.

"Whether you approve or not, it means that they have
second chance. They will live—perhaps to escape again—
and this time successfully. You, on the other hand, will b
blamed for the entire escape...." He halted and looke
pleadingly at her. "Don't you see? If you are caught, i
anything happens to you...it will...destroy me."

All at once, Emma glimpsed the anguish in his eyes. He
lips parted slightly, inviting him to kiss her.

He bent his head, and when his lips met hers, the kiss wa:
long and lingering.

At length he said, "Promise me! Promise me you'll g
back to England aboard this skiff!"

Emma made a face. "I—I—there is a problem."

"John?" Lord Brandford was certain he had anticipate
her.

"N-no."

"No? But your engagement..."

"We—we broke our engagement before he went to th
Continent."

"You did?"

"Yes."

"Then why in heaven's name didn't you tell me when —"

"It was to be a secret." Her blue eyes appealed to him. "That's why I said we had settled it before he left and that could not possibly change things."

Lord Brandford felt like tearing his hair. Yet again, he had completely misinterpreted her!

"John couldn't marry me," Emma stumbled on. "He... he t-told me that he loved Lavinia. I—I knew, of course—"

"Of course?"

Emma cast her eyes demurely downwards. "It was not my intention to eavesdrop, but I overheard them talking...."

"Harrmph! And yet you accepted his proposal—" He could not go on.

Emma flushed guiltily. "I shouldn't have done that, I know. I—I never loved him."

"You didn't?"

"Oh, no. I only accepted him in the hope that it would bring them—John and Lavinia—together."

Lord Brandford seized her and kissed her again and again, and when she looked at him at last, he was smiling.

"Yes. I see that... now." The thorns of jealousy, which had been stabbing him so unmercifully for days now, were finally withdrawn.

"I—I love you, Charles," Emma confessed. It earned her another passionate kiss—and this one was the kind that dreams are made of.

Then Lord Brandford frowned. "But if it is not John, what is the problem?"

"Clytemnestra."

Lord Brandford had not read Governor Ollivier's latest communication in *Le Moniteur*. He had no inkling, there-

fore, of the escaped prisoners' mode of transport, so th
name Clytemnestra left him totally bemused.

"I beg your pardon?"

"The donkey."

Lord Brandford was completely nonplussed. "The don
key?" he repeated stupidly.

"Yes." Emma gazed at him in eager anticipation. "Sh
is a very nice donkey—so patient, so good. Do you know
she brought us all the way from the Chateau Morphis
without a single murmur of complaint?"

Lord Brandford felt the stirrings of unease deep withi
him.

"Without Clytemnestra," continued Emma, "we woulc
never have got so far. That's why I want to take her to En
gland. I owe it to her." Her blue eyes were wide and trust
ing.

Lord Brandford gulped. "Emma...your life is in dan
ger. *Our* lives are in danger. We might be...captured by the
French, and shot." He paused and swallowed. "And you—
you are worried about a donkey?"

Emma's mouth set in an obstinate line. "I am not goin
to abandon Clytemnestra!"

"Emma, have you considered the difficulties of trans
porting her to England?"

Emma fluttered her lashes hopefully. "Couldn't we pu
her in the skiff?"

"It isn't big enough."

"Donkeys aren't very big. She would scarcely take any
more room than me."

"The skiff will only take one passenger."

"Hmm. Well perhaps we could put her in the skiff anc
send her on ahead. Then, when—"

"No!" exploded the earl.

Emma glared at him.

Lord Brandford's hands were still resting upon her shoulders, and he experienced a growing desire to shake her until her teeth rattled. He suppressed it.

"The skiff," he said, stepping away from her, "is a small fishing vessel. It isn't made for carrying donkeys."

Emma defiantly tossed her head.

"Emma, don't you see?" His palms were turned upwards in a gesture of despair. "We would need a full-scale ship for the donkey! A small skiff is just impossible!"

Mulishly, Emma dug in her heels. "I can't leave Clytemnestra behind. She wouldn't understand. She'll look at me with those big, brown, soulful eyes of hers and I shall feel dreadful. And don't tell me I'll get over it—I won't. I'll be haunted by that look for the rest of my life!"

"Emma, you have no choice. You—"

"I won't go without Clytemnestra!" declared Emma with finality.

CHAPTER FIFTEEN

LORD BRANDFORD'S HANDS were icy cold. He was trembling—not from rage, but from fear. *If Emma stays,* he reflected distractedly, *if Governor Ollivier captures her... if she is put on trial... if she is condemned...* The idea made his blood run cold.

His brain seemed frozen into immobility. He had to force himself to think logically. His brow furrowed. He paced up and down. Then gradually, the frown smoothed away.

"I have a plan!" he announced. "You will go to Dover alone.... No! Listen!" he exclaimed, as she threatened to interrupt. "Once there, you will locate my yacht, the *Venus*. Louis is in charge of her. He'll arrange to sail her across the Channel—"

Emma listened, pensively. "How big is the *Venus*?"

"Big enough to take—" Lord Brandford hesitated slightly "—a donkey."

"And the others?"

"There is room for everyone. We can all leave for England together."

Emma pursed her lips. "Suppose the others don't agree?"

His shoulders lifted slightly. "Then I shall have to come aboard the *Venus* myself with, er..."

"Clytemnestra," supplied Emma helpfully.

"Exactly. Do you accept?"

Emma considered the matter, and for one, long, terrible moment, the earl was afraid she would refuse.

Then she said, "Very well. But you'll give me your word that you won't let anything happen to Clytemnestra? You will bring her back with you on the *Venus*?"

"I give you my word."

"Thank you." Emma started to smile, then her forehead wrinkled.

"What is it?"

"Where shall I ask the *Venus* to sail to? It can't be here. Governor Ollivier is sure to be waiting."

Lord Brandford clicked his tongue in exasperation. He had forgotten that small detail. Once more he paced up and down. Finally, he spoke. "Governor Ollivier will expect us to go further along the Belgian coast. He'll assume we'll head for Holland. He'll imagine we'll count on the friendship of the Belgian and the Dutch peoples. He won't reckon on my sending for a ship from England. He'll expect us to try and hire a fishing boat in Belgium or the Low Countries... a reasonably large one, a trawler, perhaps...."

Emma nodded.

"Therefore," concluded Lord Brandford, "we shall turn back towards France. The *Venus* shall meet us at Calais."

"But that's dangerous!"

"Yes. If Governor Ollivier guesses our destination, it certainly is. However, in other respects, it is actually safer."

"Why?"

"The Channel between Dover and Calais is at its narrowest. Therefore any sea crossing will be quicker. We shall have less time to wait and we shall not be exposed on the beach so long, so our chances will be better."

"But the boats? Can they do it in the time?"

"Yves Gouleau, the master of the skiff, assures me that he can sail very quickly across the Channel. My yacht, the *Venus*, was also built for speed. With luck..."

"With luck? With a smooth sea, you mean!" cried Emma, mindful that the English Channel was notorious for its rough crossings.

"We are no longer in the period of gales," returned Lord Brandford. "The spring equinox has passed. If we had to endure that, it would be another matter. But it is May—almost June—and the weather should favour us."

"Oh, I do hope so!" declared Emma devoutly.

"Both vessels—Yves Gouleau's and mine—will be sailing at night. They will not be seen. As far as Governor Ollivier is concerned, we shall simply slip from his grasp."

WHEN EMMA HAD EXPLAINED everything to Clytemnestra, the jenny brayed. Emma offered her a comfit and insisted that she had understood.

Lord Brandford grunted. He had waited with growing impatience until Emma had finished the ritual. Then he gave her the letters he had hastily scrawled concerning Yves Gouleau and his brother, as well as the men in the Hexagon.

It was almost midnight when he took Emma by the hand and led her across the smooth sand to the water's edge. Yves Gouleau was waiting in his skiff. He looked askance at Emma. "You never said your passenger was a woman!"

"You never asked me!" retorted Lord Brandford. He pushed Emma up into the little vessel. Then he caught hold of her hand and kissed it quickly with a searing passion that left her heart crying out in pain. "Remember everything I have told you. This man is taking you to England for his brother's sake." As he spoke, he counted the fifty gold pieces out for Yves Gouleau. "He wants to free him from the hulks. It's all in the letters I gave you—"

There was time for no more. Yves Gouleau was in haste to depart. The wind was blowing lightly to the northwest, and his sail swelled with the breeze.

The Earl of Brandford stood knee deep in the water, watching while the skiff's prow cut a swathe through the waves towards Dover.

LORD DRUCE WAS WAITING for him when he returned to the Hexagon.

"Everything all right, Charles?"

"Perfect," responded Lord Brandford. "It couldn't have gone better."

"Good." Viscount Zellinge was on his feet. "Now that she's gone, we can get rid of that wretched, flea-ridden donkey!" He picked up a rifle and headed purposely for Clytemnestra's abode.

Lord Druce forestalled him by raising a pistol and aiming it at Viscount Zellinge's head.

"Miss Armstead wants the donkey. As long as I am here to have a say in it, she shall have the donkey."

Lord Zellinge cursed him roundly.

The Earl of Brandford, supporting Lord Druce with his gun, smiled in a coldly superior fashion. "I think you owe her that much, Zellinge. All of you do!"

"Now look here—" began Lord Zellinge.

"No, you look," interrupted the earl. "If you don't wish to fall in with my plan, you are not obliged to. You may leave here now and go wherever it is you wish to go. But that donkey and I are returning to England together—"

"And so am I!" added Lord Druce. "The rest of you can come with us, or—" He stopped himself before he finished with, —or go to hell!

Viscount Zellinge declared sourly that he didn't like Emma, that he didn't like Lord Brandford, that he didn't like Lord Druce and that he detested Clytemnestra. Furthermore, he maintained that Lord Brandford's plan was doomed to failure, and he, for one, was not going to be sent back to the Chateau Morphise—or the galleys, come to that. He had a much better idea.

"We'll go inland. Governor Ollivier will never anticipate that. We'll head south. We'll go through Austria to Trieste. I have friends who managed to escape that way. There are people I know of whom we can ask for help."

"If they haven't changed sides by this time," sneered Ivor Jones.

A roar of fury came from one of the other men. Ivor Jones responded with an angry bellow. Within seconds, a fierce argument was raging.

Lord Brandford sat down on one of the more comfortable chairs. It was, as he could very well see, going to be a tediously long night.

AT SOME POINT, Lord Brandford had fallen asleep. He woke with a start. He couldn't say exactly what had wakened him.

Clytemnestra was happily munching some hay, with Lord Druce asleep at her feet, one of his legs resting on a bale of straw, and the other sprawled across the floor. His head was on the seat of one of the chairs, and he looked extremely uncomfortable. The rest of the group were also fast asleep.

Lord Brandford stood up. His body ached. He pulled aside one of the shutters and looked out. The early-morning sun was shining brightly. It had rained during the night, though. The rhythm of the raindrops had sent him to sleep—that and complete exhaustion.

Lord Brandford walked to the rear of the Hexagon and gazed out to sea. The rain had washed Emma's tracks away. He smiled and rejoined the others.

The problem of who went where had been settled at last. Lord Zellinge was going to lead the main party south via Austria to Trieste. Lord Druce, Lord Brandford and Ivor Jones were, however, going to go to Calais, with Clytemnestra in tow, to meet the *Venus*.

"Well, if that's what you want," said Lord Brandford, "I wish you the best of luck." There were general expressions of goodwill, and everyone shook hands.

They had just finished collecting their gear and were about to depart, when Ivor Jones, white-faced, came hurtling down from one of the Hexagon's turrets.

"The French! The bloody French! They're crawling all over the place!" He rounded on Lord Zellinge. "It's your fault entirely, you painted dandy! If you hadn't sat there arguing your silly foppish head off, we would have been out of here by now!"

"You Welsh clodhopper!" Lord Zellinge retorted, stung. "You scum! How dare you talk to me like that!"

The men were immediately divided into two camps: those who were for attacking Lord Zellinge, and those who were for defending him. Every voice was raised. Then suddenly, there was a dull thud against the door, which announced the arrival of Governor Ollivier. His soldiers were battering it down.

The Earl of Brandford acted swiftly. He smashed one of the window panes and fired a shot. The result was marvellous to behold. Some fifty Frenchmen ran for cover like so many beetles. As they took refuge behind the sand dunes, a cheer went up from the escaped prisoners.

Lord Druce glared at them. "You fatheads! We may have driven the French back, but we can't keep them off forever! We're trapped. We'll either have to surrender...or be killed!"

HIS MAJESTY'S FRIGATE *Eurydice* was patrolling the seas east of Dover and the Cinque Ports. The night had been peaceful. Now it was dawn.

"Sail to starboard, sir!" an able-bodied seaman addressed the captain.

Captain Coates took his telescope and surveyed the bounding main. "A skiff," he remarked laconically. "Two people. Could be French. Let's take a closer look."

"Aye-aye, sir."

YVES GOULEAU COULD ALREADY see white cliffs in the distance. England. He smiled. Then he spotted the frigate bearing down upon him. It was a military vessel, armed to the teeth.

Emma saw his face fall. "What is it?"

"There!" He pointed at the *Eurydice*. "We must get out of here!" He put his hand to the tiller.

Emma stayed him. "Wait!" Her sharp eyes scanned the frigate from prow to stern. She smiled. "It's carrying the Union Jack. It's British. We're safe."

"You, maybe," began Gouleau, "but if they take me, one of the enemy..."

Emma patted his gnarled hand reassuringly. "Don't forget, I have letters concerning you. And we are not being taken. We are coming in voluntarily."

Yves Gouleau blinked. "P-pardon?"

"Make straight for it."

He drew in his breath making a hissing sound. Then he calculated his chances of outrunning the *Eurydice*, and concluded that it was impossible. He snorted disgustedly. "I hope you know what you are doing, *mademoiselle*!"

THE FIRST LIEUTENANT of the *Eurydice* saluted. "They are making straight for us, sir."

"Interesting," returned Captain Coates.

It was not many moments later that the *Eurydice* met Yves Gouleau's skiff. Owner and passenger came aboard, and the skiff was taken in tow. Emma and Yves Gouleau were presented to Captain Coates, who bowed with that formal correctness for which the Royal Navy is noted.

"Miss Armstead. Delighted. Mr. Gouleau..."

Emma smiled charmingly. Yves Gouleau scowled sullenly.

"Mr. Gouleau has been conducting me to Dover," explained Emma. "We are on an important mission..." And mindful of the missive Lord Druce had pressed upon her, she added, "For the Prince Regent."

Captain Coates was sceptical. "Do you have any, um, proof of this?"

"Oh, yes. I have letters from Lord Druce and Lord Brandford."

"I see." Captain Coates cleared his throat. "May I see the dispatches?"

FORTUNATELY FOR EMMA, Captain Coates had received detailed instructions from the Admiralty concerning Lord Druce and Lord Brandford. A careful perusal of her letters showed him at once where his duty lay.

As soon as he could, he rejoined his guests.

"We are indebted to you...both," he assured them, remembering just in time to include Yves Gouleau. "Naturally we will bring you to your destination. We cannot escort you back...at least, not into French waters. But we may be able to accompany the *Venus* part of the way across the Channel."

THE MORNING SUN CAST its golden rays across the white cliffs of Dover. Louis de Troyes was fast asleep in his cabin on the *Venus*. He was dreaming, a deliciously sweet dream in which Lady Marcella was in his arms. They were making love....

A loud crash awakened him, as Emma burst into his cabin, slamming the door behind her with a deafening thud. "Louis! Wake up!"

Louis de Troyes's beautiful dream was fading, and he was reluctant to let it go. He grunted unwelcomingly at Emma, turned away from her and tried with all his might to recapture it.

"Louis, get up this instant!" She seized his hand and started to drag him from his bunk.

Her determination made an impact on him. His eyes widened with shock. He snatched his hand from her grasp and pulled the white sheet up to his neck. "Emma! What are you doing in my cabin?"

"I had to come. There is no time to lose. You have to get up now. The *Venus* must sail for France directly!"

Louis de Troyes, still hanging tightly on to the sheet with one hand, ran his free hand confusedly through his sleep-tousled hair. He realized in dismay that he was no longer dreaming, and that Emma was actually in his cabin. Thank heaven she had shut the door behind her!

"Emma, that is impossible!" he remonstrated. "We cannot depart forthwith!"

Emma glared at him. "Why not?"

"There are the small matters of getting the crew on board, of the tide, and—"

"Tsk!" Emma clicked her tongue in exasperation. "Never mind. Whatever has to be done, do it without delay. Charles is in terrible danger, and so is John and the other people with them. If the *Venus* does not sail immediately, they are done for!"

Louis de Troyes blinked at her.

"You must go to Calais! Here! Read Charles's letter!" She thrust it at him.

Holding the sheet between his teeth, Louis de Troyes took the letter from her and slit it open. Then he read it through, being careful all the while not to lower his guard. Soon he was muttering imprecations under his breath: a fine pickle Lord Druce and Lord Brandford had landed in!

Emma was speaking again. "Charles found a man—Yves Gouleau—who was willing to bring me to England. His skiff is small. It would only take one passenger. I've sent him to Lady Brandford. Charles said she was here in Dover with Marcella."

Louis de Troyes stared at her as if mesmerized. "You—you sent a common sailor...to Lady Brandford...as a guest...at this hour of the morning?"

"Yes, of course." Emma was unperturbed. "Yves Gouleau helped me because he wants to free his brother, Aristide, who is in the hulks. Captain Coates, who picked us up, said he would write to the Admiralty and ask for their help. So it is practically settled, but I thought Yves Gouleau should stay with Lady Brandford. It would give weight to his case."

"Yes. No doubt." The audacity of it left Louis de Troyes gasping.

"She will help, won't she?"

"She—" he fished about for the right words "—she will move heaven and earth to have this business dealt with quickly."

"Oh, good." Emma was relieved. "I'm so glad. Yves Gouleau is a bit dour, but he grows on one. I'd like to see his brother set at liberty."

"You needn't worry." Louis de Troyes was now fully awake. He realized that the Admiralty would act even faster than Lady Brandford. It would be a day—two or three at the most—before Aristide Gouleau had his freedom.

Emma suddenly became aware that despite her exhortations, Louis de Troyes was still in bed. "Louis, for heaven's sake, don't dawdle! There is no time to lose. You must get up. Now!"

Louis de Troyes eyed her balefully. "I can't."

"Why not?"

"Because you are in my cabin."

"Pshaw!"

"Emma, it was a hot night last night...."

Emma gazed uncomprehendingly at him.

"Emma, I went to sleep...naked."

CHAPTER SIXTEEN

"LOUIS!" LADY BRANDFORD cried, embracing him warmly. "You don't know what kind of a morning I have had!"

Louis de Troyes led her across the freshly scrubbed deck of the *Venus*. The crew were preparing to hoist sail, and in a few minutes the anchor would be raised and the yacht would be under way.

"I can imagine!" he commiserated. "Emma came to visit me—"

"Did she tell you she is no longer engaged to John?"

He shook his head. "No. She said not a word."

"Harrmph! Well, apparently they broke their engagement before he went to the Continent."

"Astounding! So now Emma and John are not going to be married—nor are Charles and Lavinia!"

"Exactly!" Lady Brandford threw her hands up in the air. Then, as the ship lurched, she gripped Louis de Troyes's arm again—very tightly. "And to think, we have had all that worry simply because the four of them didn't know their own minds!"

"It is too bad of them!"

"Yes, it is. Ah, well," she continued with a shrug, "at least they have finally come to their senses."

"Er, yes."

"That is not all," continued Lady Brandford feelingly. "Did Emma tell you she sent a sailor—a common, scruffy *French* sailor, Yves Gouleau by name—to me?"

"She did. Apparently, Charles persuaded him to take her to England. He did it because he wants to free his brother."

"So I understand." The scent of lavender wafted across the deck. "It has been confirmed now, thank goodness. Lord Keith was wonderful! So was the Prince Regent! Aristide Gouleau is to be released by the weekend."

"Not sooner?"

"No."

They were in the captain's cabin now. Lady Brandford ignored the charts and papers scattered across the oaken table, and sat down in a maroon leather-upholstered armchair.

"Lord Keith suggested that we wait until the *Venus* has had a chance to collect Charles and John." She smiled winningly. "I have given Yves Gouleau some tea and some sugar to take home. He seemed rather pleased."

Louis de Troyes smiled, too. Not only were these items expensive, but they were—thanks to Napoleon's Continental System—extremely difficult to obtain in Europe.

Their appearance in the hands of Yves Gouleau would suggest to his neighbours that he had been indulging in some acceptable smuggling rather than in some unacceptable fraternizing with the enemy.

"I am sure he was," murmured Louis de Troyes.

"I'm glad you think so. Incidentally, where is Emma?"

"She went to London to make sure all goes well for Yves Gouleau. He does not speak any English, you know. She felt he should be, er, protected, until he and his brother can sail once more."

"Very decent of her. Now tell me, Louis, why did you ask me to come aboard?"

Louis de Troyes sighed. "So that I could return Marcella to your care."

Lady Brandford blanched. "M-Marcella?"

"Yes. Me." Lady Marcella came into the cabin, shooting wounded glances at her lover and her mother. "He told me I couldn't come with him. I am to go home and wait there like a good girl."

"Marcella!" Louis de Troyes cried despairingly. "I—I didn't say anything of the kind!"

"No," grumbled Lady Marcella, "but you meant it that way."

"I did not! I was considering your reputation! Your honour!"

Lady Marcella pouted and sank into another maroon leather armchair. Her limpid brown eyes were fixed appealingly on her mother. "He is going into danger. He could be wounded...or killed. I wanted to be by his side, where I belong but—" She stopped and bit her lip.

Lady Brandford looked from one to the other. She sighed deeply. "I should never have listened to Charles!"

Louis de Troyes stared at her. "W-what do you m-mean?"

"Charles is a good son, a fine brother. But he is not a father. He has never been a father. He does not have the instincts of a parent." She sniffed. "I should have trusted *my* instincts."

"M-Mother dear?" questioned Lady Marcella.

"It is time you two were married," stated Lady Brandford.

"B-but," stammered Louis de Troyes, hardly daring to believe his ears, "surely Ch-charles m-must give his c-consent?"

Lady Brandford shook her head. "Charles isn't Marcella's guardian. I am. My consent will be enough."

Lady Marcella gave a scream of delight and threw herself into her mother's arms.

Louis de Troyes kissed his future mother-in-law's hands as tears spilled from his eyes.

"But," stipulated Lady Brandford, "it must be done properly. You will come to London with me at once, Marcella, and we'll begin making the arrangements. Then, when you come back from France, Louis, you may set the date. What do you say?"

"Lady Brandford, I don't know what to say." Louis de Troyes was beside himself with joy.

"You could start by calling me 'Mother dear' and giving me a kiss." She offered him her cheek.

"Thank you, Mother dear." He kissed her affectionately.

"Marcella? Does this meet with your approval?"

"Oh, yes! Yes! Yes!" cried her daughter.

THE HEXAGON WAS UNDER SIEGE, shots had been exchanged and both sides were taking stock of the situation. Then, as the sun started to climb high in the heavens, a man with a white flag was seen advancing across the sand.

"Hold your fire!" commanded Lord Druce.

Xavier Roos wore a *tricouleur* sash over his beige cloth coat. He spoke English, French and Flemish. That was why he had been selected by Governor Ollivier to deliver his message to the beleaguered defenders of the Hexagon.

He read it in flat, unemotional tones. "'You are surrounded. There is no hope of escape. If you surrender now, your lives will be spared. If you do not, it will only be a matter of time before you are either starved into submission or shot. You have two hours to make up your minds. The choice is yours.'

"It is signed," announced Xavier Roos, coming closer, "Ollivier, Governor of the Chateau Morphise." There was a short pause. "May I enter and give you the proclamation?"

Permission was given and Xavier Roos stepped inside the Hexagon.

The proclamation was duly scrutinized.

"What shall I tell Governor Ollivier?" asked Xavier Roos.

"Tell him to go to hell!" snapped Lord Zellinge.

There was a general murmur of agreement.

"You are determined to hold out? You will not reconsider?"

Ivor Jones looked as if he were about to spit on the man. Lord Brandford restrained him. "We have no intention of surrendering to Governor Ollivier."

Xavier Roos blinked.

"He's sizing us up!" said Lord Zellinge suddenly.

Xavier Roos's countenance was a shade too innocent.

"You should never have let him in here!" fumed Lord Zellinge. His eyes flashed at Lord Brandford and Lord Druce. "Do you know what he will do? He'll report to Governor Ollivier on everything he finds here, the dirty little French—"

"Enough!" cried Lord Brandford.

"Tell Governor Ollivier," said Lord Druce, "that he may have us boxed in here for the present, but we got out of the Chateau Morphise and we'll get out of this trap, too, somehow!"

"Aye. Aye. Aye," seconded the men.

Xavier Roos pursed his lips and folded his hands in front of him. "You have no hope of leaving here. There is no way through the French cordon."

A hissing sound came from the men, but Lord Druce, taking his cue from Lord Brandford, checked them.

"Even if you were to escape," continued Xavier Roos, "where would you go? South to Trieste?"

"How the deuce . . . ?" began Lord Zellinge.

"Governor Ollivier considered that was the most likely possibility," stated Xavier Roos. "It is logical, you see.

Others have escaped successfully by that route, so—"
Phlegmatically he lifted his shoulders.

"So he thinks we'll try it," concluded Lord Druce. "That means he'll have it watched...."

"Naturally," confirmed Xavier Roos.

"And if we follow it, we'll be sunk!"

Xavier Roos nodded unconcernedly.

The men looked disgusted. Whatever happened now, Lord Zellinge's plan to make for Trieste would have to be abandoned, there was no question about that.

Lord Brandford frowned. *Rum fellow this Xavier Roos,* he mused. *Why is he telling us this?* Simply to frighten them? Or did he have another reason? Xavier Roos was Governor Ollivier's messenger... or was he?

Or is he, wondered the earl, *also here on his own account?* He hardly dared hope such a thing. Surely it was too good to be true... and yet... and yet... Was he in this roundabout manner trying to tell them he was a friend? The chance could not be missed. The earl decided to play his hunch.

"If we were to escape," he remarked casually, "we would return directly to England, across the Channel."

There was a gasp from the others at this unexpected revelation.

Lord Brandford made a sign for them to be silent.

Xavier Roos snorted. "No fishing vessel would take you."

"We won't need one."

A strange gleam appeared in Xavier Roos's eyes. "You—you have the means... to get back to England without outside help?"

Lord Brandford nodded in assent.

The others were quiet. What was the earl up to?

"You are joking," said Xavier Roos.

"Of course, he is," laughed Lord Zellinge. "He—"

"No, I'm not," interrupted Lord Brandford.

He was certain now, for he had heard just the slightest note in Xavier Roos's voice which told him that his guess was right: this man was not an enemy.

"You can take," Xavier Roos countered disbelievingly, "eleven men...?"

"More than that."

Their eyes met.

"You—you are serious?" Xavier Roos's voice quavered slightly. "This—this is not...a trick?"

"No."

"You give me your word?"

"As an officer and a gentleman."

Xavier Roos expelled a sigh. "I thank you."

Tensely, everyone waited to hear what he would say next.

"If I—" he licked his suddenly dry lips "—if I were to show you a way out of here... You would take three more passengers?"

"Gladly," agreed Lord Brandford.

"Now just a minute..." protested Lord Zellinge.

"Pack it in," advised Lord Druce. "It's his ship. If he wants to take on a few more passengers—"

"But they might be spies!"

"Don't be an idiot!"

"I think," said Lord Zellinge with great dignity, "that we should know more about these passengers before we risk taking them with us."

"Of course, of course," replied Xavier Roos, eyeing Lord Brandford with a mixture of hope and incredulity. "The passengers...if I can satisfy you...you will take them?"

"Yes," answered the earl.

"You promise?"

"I give you my word."

Xavier Roos looked as if he had been freed from eternal torment. "Gentlemen. Your pardon." He mopped his brow. "I—I am a poor man. I am a peaceable man. I live with my wife and our son in a house nearby. I fish for a living, and my wife keeps chickens. My son—he is only a boy—learns to be a watchmaker. But he is big for his age." He paused and shuddered.

"I—I have an enemy. He has told people my son is eighteen. I learned—" tears streamed suddenly down his leathery cheeks "—I learned from a distant cousin of mine that they are going to conscript my son."

Murmurs of sympathy came from his audience.

"My wife...my wife, she notices that the troops are going east." Xavier Roos went on. "She says Napoleon intends to fight Russia. Do you know what it is like to fight in Russia? My wife, Tania, she is Russian. She says our son will certainly die." Xavier Roos almost choked with emotion "Piet is only fourteen, a mere child. He is too young...too young to die."

"So you wish us to take you and your wife and son to England with us," remarked Lord Brandford. "And in return, you will show us how to get out of the Hexagon?"

Xavier Roos nodded and dried his eyes.

"I accept." Lord Brandford offered the man his hand. "What about the rest of you?"

"Most certainly, and with all my heart!" exclaimed Lord Druce.

The others gave their assent, and even Lord Zellinge, grudgingly, was in accord.

Xavier Roos smiled tremulously. "A thousand thanks." He bowed low. "I shall return now to Governor Ollivier. I shall then come and lead you out of here by means of a secret passage. Be patient."

"One moment..." Lord Brandford, in high spirits, stayed him. "What do you say," he asked the others, "shall we give Governor Ollivier an even chance?"

"WELL?" DEMANDED Governor Ollivier.

Xavier Roos wrung his hands. "The English...they say

ou have given them too much time. If you allow them two
ours, they will escape."

Governor Ollivier laughed heartily. "Listen to that! These
mad English! They know we have them cornered, and they
oke about it!"

His subordinates joined him in his merriment, but when
he laughter had died down, Governor Ollivier again turned
o Xavier Roos. "Go and tell them they will have until two.
That is so that we can have a decent lunch. But—" he wag-
gled his finger ferociously "—if they don't surrender then,
we will blast them to kingdom come!"

"IT IS SETTLED." Xavier Roos had carried out his second
visit to the Hexagon. "I have given them your instructions,
Governor Ollivier."

"Excellent. You may go home now."

Xavier Roos bowed and lumbered slowly in the direction
of his house. His wife was waiting for him. As soon as he
was inside he said, "Get Piet!"

Tania Roos eyed her husband shrewdly. "What is it?"

"I have no time to explain. Don't bother with lunch. Just
take what you can carry and meet me by the stone cross on
the beach. And Tania—make sure the French don't see
you!"

"WHAT WE NEED NOW," remarked Lord Brandford, "is a
diversion. Something to keep Governor Ollivier occupied
when he comes in here."

Viscount Zellinge snorted. "There is nothing to make a
diversion with!"

"Of course there is," disagreed Lord Druce. "We have
furniture, guns, candles, string—"

"And then," added Dick Moss, "there is always the
wine."

"What wine?" enquired the earl.

"I found some old bottles of wine in the cellar. I tasted one, and it was musty. I tried another, but it was as sour as old vinegar. I imagine the whole lot is useless—for drinking. But wine bottles popping... well, that's another matter."

Lord Druce smiled. "Why not?"

The eleven of them set to work. Furniture had to be set up, candles placed strategically under the wine bottles. The idea was that at the moment of their departure, the candles would be lit. The flames would heat the wine. When Governor Ollivier and his men came in, the corks would pop....

"It all depends on the timing," declared Dick Moss. He had been in the Royal Engineers and knew about such things.

The Earl of Brandford consulted the plain fob he had used since his arrival in France. "It is nearly half-past one now."

Lord Zellinge clicked his tongue. "Where is Xavier Roos? He should have been here by now." He paced disconsolately up and down. "I think that rotten Belgian has abandoned us. There is no way out. He was teasing us. He—"

He was in the middle of pouring out all his disaffection, when a shower of plaster and paper cascaded into the room and, dusty and panting, Xavier Roos appeared through the hole he had created.

The eleven men stared at him as if he were an apparition. Who would have thought that a tunnel would come straight into the room like that?

Viscount Zellinge recovered first. "You took your time!"

Xavier Roos was offended. "The tunnel is a mile long. I had to go out of my way—home first—and then by a roundabout route to the entrance, so I would not be seen."

Lord Druce frowned. "Does anyone else know of this tunnel?"

Xavier Roos shook his head. "I only know about it because my grandfather worked here. When I was a child, he told me about it, and he took me to the entrance. He showed me how it went for a mile under the beach."

Lord Zellinge gave a derisory laugh. "He is a local. If he knows about it, the entire countryside—"

"Monsieur!" Xavier Roos was dignity personified. "You flatter me! I am as much a stranger here as you. I am a Fleming. This is a French community. I only came here with my wife and son to find work. I have worked in many places, *monsieur*. Including England."

"But your grandfather..."

"My grandfather has been dead these forty years. There is no one here now who remembers the Hexagon. I have heard them talking, believe me, and no one apart from myself knows about the tunnel."

"But—"

"We are wasting time," said Lord Brandford. "We still have to sweep this mess up so Governor Ollivier and his men don't see it. We must put something in front of that hole to hide it and light the candles under the wine bottles. Then we can go."

They set to work with a will, and in a matter of minutes had cleaned away the powdery debris. A large armoire was selected for covering the hole. Then one by one, the candles were lit.

"Are we ready?" asked Xavier Roos.

"Yes," answered Lord Druce.

"Excellent!" He stepped into the tunnel.

The others started to follow him.

Lord Brandford took hold of Clytemnestra's rope bridle.

Viscount Zellinge stared openmouthed. "You are *not* taking *that*!"

Lord Brandford sighed. "Yes. I am."

"You can't be serious!"

"Zellinge, if you don't mind, we'll postpone this discussion until later."

Having bribed Clytemnestra with a comfit, the earl entered the tunnel, and the armoire was pulled over the entrance after him.

CHAPTER SEVENTEEN

DESPITE THE COMFITS, Clytemnestra was not pleased with the tunnel. It was dark, damp and foul-smelling. Clytemnestra was particular about the air she breathed, and she ventured her protests with loud braying.

"I wish that bloody donkey would shut up!" hissed Lord Zellinge. There was no response.

"Can't you do anything about it, Brandford?"

"She'll be fine when we get out," the earl replied soothingly.

"Ought to be shot! Mangy, noisy beast! It'll give us all away!"

Clytemnestra sensed Lord Zellinge's hostility, and resented it, so she did the only thing a well-bred donkey can do in the circumstances. She lifted up her dainty hooves and gave him a sharp kick.

Lord Zellinge roared with indignation as he was knocked off balance and fell into the damp slime that formed the tunnel floor.

"That'll teach you!" cried Ivor Jones.

"Never insult a lady!" exclaimed Dick Moss.

"Are you all right, Zellinge?" enquired Lord Druce.

"Come, let me help you up," offered Lord Brandford.

Lord Zellinge, winded and muttering curses, was helped to his feet. There was nothing broken, but he was bruised. He limped on at a respectful distance behind the donkey. Although he said no more about shooting her, Dick Moss thought he heard the viscount murmur a few decidedly uncomplimentary words about her origins.

THEY EMERGED FROM THE TUNNEL well out of sight of Governor Ollivier and his troops. Xavier Roos knelt in the sand and crossed himself, and Lord Brandford at once saw why: in front of them was a large, weatherbeaten stone cross, encircled on top by a stone halo.

It must have been here for centuries! reflected Lord Brandford as he gazed in fascination and awe at the unreadable characters on its base.

From behind the cross, Madame Roos and her son emerged. Lord Brandford saw at once why Xavier Roos had been worried: Piet Roos was tall and strong for his age, more than five foot ten and still growing. For all his youth, he had the form of an adult.

"Are you all right, Xavier?" asked Madame Roos.

"Yes." Xavier Roos stood up, brushing the sand from his trousers. "Gentlemen, my wife." The men murmured some words of respect, and those who had hats removed them. "My son." Greetings were exchanged.

"We must hurry," said Lord Brandford. "We still have a long way to go, and if the French catch us, we are done for."

"Oh, they won't find us here, surely?" Lord Zellinge, as changeable as a weathercock, had recovered his good spirits.

Lord Druce grimaced. "I hope not. But it is as well to take precautions. We must make sure there are no tracks. Madame Roos, perhaps you would like to sit on the donkey?"

All eyes at once turned to look for Clytemnestra. She had come out of the tunnel, and it was then she had seen the sand, acres and acres of silver sand. Joyfully she had trotted towards it. Now she lay on her back, happily rolling in it.

Lord Brandford convinced her to stand up, and as Tania Roos mounted her, Clytemnestra was surprisingly cooperative. She did not bray once. Indeed, she was happy to be gone from the Hexagon and its dank, dark tunnel. Lord Brandford had no difficulty leading her along the beach in the direction of Calais, with Xavier Roos and his son Piet following.

The rest of the men, meanwhile, swept away all tracks leading from the tunnel entrance to the water's edge. As they reached the sea, they took advantage of the incoming tide by walking on the damp sand and left the waves to wash away any footprints for them.

Lord Brandford glanced at his fob. "It is a little after two. Governor Ollivier will be breaking into the Hexagon about now. When he finds us gone, he'll train his telescope upon the beach. If we are not beyond its range, he will be after us!"

GOVERNOR OLLIVIER CONSULTED his watch, and determined that it was exactly two o'clock. He put his telescope to his eye, but there was no white flag visible at the Hexagon. He shut his telescope with a snap and summoned one of his subordinates.

"Call upon the English to surrender."

The officer, who had a very loud voice, stepped forward and bellowed, *"Surrender!"*

There was no answer.

"Surrender or prepare to die!"

Still no answer.

"Shall we send for Xavier Roos to parley with them again?" enquired one of the French.

Governor Ollivier considered. "No. That will not be necessary. We have given them enough time. Advance!"

To the muffled beating of drums, the French closed in, forming a blue noose which slowly tightened around the neck of the Hexagon, but there was no response from the men within.

Governor Ollivier was puzzled. He suspected a trap. "Shoot the lock off the door. Then break it down. But be careful. One does not know what these devious English may be up to!"

The door gave way quite easily. The French, with their rifles at the ready, swept into the Hexagon.

"But there is no one here!" they cried. "The place is empty!"

"Nonsense! We had the place surrounded. How could they have escaped?"

"Yet they have vanished into thin air!"

"Perhaps," suggested Governor Ollivier dryly, "they are hiding upstairs or in the cellars. Start a search."

The French swarmed all over the Hexagon. Suddenly, there was a series of explosions.

"Treachery!" cried the searchers as they fired at their unseen foes. "We are betrayed!"

It was some minutes before the explosions died down and the smoke from their rifles cleared away. Half a dozen Frenchmen were found lying on the ground, their eyes closed, their limbs motionless, but of the beleaguered defenders there was no sign.

"Murderers!" cried the French. "Cowardly dogs!"

Tenderly they knelt beside their fallen comrades, observing the red substance which was oozing from their mouths.

But it was not blood—it was wine, for in spite of what Dick Moss believed, some of the wine in the cellar was rather good. Those Frenchmen who had been knocked to the ground had made this pleasant discovery. *Why waste good wine?* they had asked themselves, as they lay flat on their backs with their mouths open, and took advantage of the situation.

Governor Ollivier was not impressed. After reprimanding his men for drunkenness, he declared, "The English must be somewhere. They did not break through our cordon, so they must still be here. I want this place torn apart. Find them!" Impatiently, he glanced again at his watch. It was already ten minutes to three.

Another fifteen minutes passed before someone looked in the armoire. It was empty. With a carelessness born of frustration, the man slammed the door too hard, and the armoire toppled over, revealing the tunnel.

Governor Ollivier was informed at once.

"So!" His face was red with anger. "Another of their tricks! I should have guessed! I should have realized when they sent that message through Xavier Roos that they were up to something!" He swore under his breath. Then his black eyes were on his officers. "I want some men to find out where the tunnel goes. I want a detachment to go along the beach and tell me if there is any sign of the fugitives. I want a good rider to take my horse to the nearest town and tell them to send me the *tirailleurs*.

"I will teach those vile English to play tricks on me!" exclaimed Governor Ollivier, as his men scurried away to do his bidding.

BY FOUR O'CLOCK, Governor Ollivier's orders had been carried out in full. The tunnel was found to be a mile in length; to reach the stone cross; to have access to the beach and to a main road. With the aid of telescopes, the road and the beach were carefully scanned, but the fugitives were not to be seen.

Governor Ollivier was unperturbed. The *tirailleurs* had arrived. These cavalrymen were the most relentless pursuers, the best trackers in the whole French army. Their name alone struck terror into the hearts of all deserters and of all escaping prisoners. Whichever way the English go, decided Governor Ollivier, they are lost!

"The *tirailleurs*," he ordered, "will divide into four groups. Two groups will take the road. Two groups will take the beach. Thus every direction will be covered."

He glanced approvingly at the *tirailleurs* with their smart uniforms and their gleaming sabres. He smiled to himself.

Being mounted, the *tirailleurs* could travel at a rate of eight to twelve miles an hour where the fugitives, on foot, could reach a speed of only four to five miles an hour.

"We shall have news of the English by nightfall," he predicted. "We shall have them back in custody by dawn."

CHAPTER EIGHTEEN

LORD BRANDFORD CONSULTED his fob: it was half-past four. If he had been in England, he would have been finishing tea just now. He glanced at the sun. The heat had parched his throat. He would have liked a cup of tea, but there was no time to sit down and brew some.

He and his party had covered about nine miles since they had left the tunnel.

"How I should love to rest!" declared Viscount Zelinge.

"We can't afford to," returned the earl.

"We're not out of the woods yet," added Lord Druce. "Governor Ollivier is not to be underestimated. He is thorough."

"Yes, he is," agreed Lord Brandford, struck by the thought that if Governor Ollivier were to send horsemen looking for them, he could still catch them.

Fear spurred him on.

LOUIS DE TROYES STOOD on the deck of the *Venus*, watching as the white cliffs of Dover receded. His grey eyes were fastened on Lady Marcella. She was standing at the dockside, waving frantically. She kept on waving a pretty scarlet handkerchief until Lady Brandford fairly dragged her away.

A smile touched Louis de Troyes's lips. *When we return, my darling,* he thought blissfully, *we shall be married at last!* And that sweet dream he had this very morning would become a reality!

The English Channel was as smooth as glass, and all sails were unfurled to catch the least whisper of the wind.

Then a breeze began to stir. It grew stronger as the sun disappeared behind black clouds, and the sails were hauled down. It began to rain.

THE BREEZE WHICH WAS pushing the *Venus* on her way to France, was also making itself felt along the Belgian coast-line, whipping the sand up along the beach, blowing it into a cloud of knives.

The *tirailleurs'* horses were flayed alive. In order to keep their seats, they had to go inland. They knew the move would slow them down, but they were not unduly worried, for they had made good time. Besides, their quarry was on foot . . . and it was still light.

THE SAND CUT INTO EVERYONE'S flesh. Lord Brandford, like the others, shielded his face with his arm.

I had no idea sand could be so painful! he reflected rue-fully, wishing he could take shelter until the wind died down. But they could not stop; they had to keep on going, sand or no sand.

Clytemnestra protested loudly. Lord Brandford spoke soothingly to her. Offering her another comfit, he pulled her forward, and somewhat dubiously, she followed him.

THE SANDSTORM QUIETED suddenly. Then it started to rain: not a quiet, gentle rain, but a heavy downpour.

The *tirailleurs* came across a farmhouse. As it was a French farmhouse, they were made welcome. There was an offer of onion soup with cheese floating on top, and red wine was served to wash down some freshly baked bread. A log fire was lit to take the chill off the air. Monsieur and madame begged them to stay and dry their clothes.

FOR LORD BRANDFORD and the others, there was no welcoming farmhouse; no hot soup; no warm fire; no wine; no bread. On the contrary, they were soaked through to the skin. They shivered. They felt like drowned rats. But they had to keep on going towards their destination, the beaches flanking Calais.

NIGHT HAD FALLEN. The storm was over now. The clouds had gone. Stars twinkled in the sky above. A full moon cast its light upon the shore.

Louis de Troyes was on the deck of the *Venus*. For almost an hour he had stood motionless, his eyes scanning the coastline. Suddenly he cried, "There she is!"

The white statue of Sainte Marguerite with her arms outstretched towards the sea, her feet covered with flowers, was clearly visible. A cheer went up from the men.

"We'll drop anchor then, Mr. Kedge," he addressed his second-in-command. "Lower the longboat."

LORD BRANDFORD STUMBLED along the beach with Clytemnestra behind him, and the others staggering along as best they could. Suddenly, out of the corner of his eye, he caught a gleam of white.

He halted. "Sainte Marguerite!" he gasped joyfully, as the statue seemed to smile at him.

"There she is! Our landmark!" Lord Brandford sank to his knees. "Exactly as I wrote to Louis!" He laughed aloud. "We've made it!" Again he glanced at his fob. In the moonlight he could make out the time. "It is exactly midnight. We can rest now."

The others stopped. Their legs gave way under them, and they sank onto the wet sand.

Lord Brandford gazed out to sea, watching the moon cast a yellow ribbon of light across the waves. And in its beam he saw the lines of a sailing ship—a yacht.

"The *Venus*!" His voice was hoarse. "She's here already! She must have had the wind behind her all the way!"

"It's just as well," murmured Lord Druce. "I wouldn't fancy our chances if we had to wait here!"

The beach was exposed, and they were vulnerable. Calais itself was too close for comfort. However, there was no sign of the French—yet.

AT THE HEXAGON, Governor Ollivier was receiving reports from the *tirailleurs*. These were negative: no escaped prisoners; no English. He frowned. "That means they have gone in the direction of Calais."

"But that is madness!" cried one of his subordinates.

"Or extreme cunning," retorted Governor Ollivier. "If they have arranged a rendezvous with a ship—an English ship—" He paused and tapped his fingers impatiently upon a rickety table, where a map of the coastline was spread before him. Abruptly he turned to the commanders of the *tirailleurs*. "Remount! We go to Calais!"

"SHIP AHOY! SHIP AHOY!"

"It's them!" Louis de Troyes knew that no Frenchman would use that cry. He leapt out of the longboat to embrace Lord Brandford and Lord Druce in turn. "I am so glad to see you both!"

"Not as glad as we are to see *you*!" responded the others.

"Were you followed?" questioned Louis de Troyes.

"We suspect we are being pursued," replied Lord Druce, "although we haven't seen any sign of them."

Louis de Troyes needed to hear no more. "In that case, we must get you out of here quickly. Who shall be first into the longboat?"

They took Tania and Piet Roos first, as well as two of the men—those who were most fatigued.

As the longboat started back to the *Venus*, Lord Brandford cleared his throat. "Ahem! There is one small thing...."

"Yes?" enquired Louis de Troyes.

"Er, do we have a raft aboard?"

"A raft? What for?"

Lord Brandford extended his hand. There, contentedly munching the flowers and the grass around the statue of Sainte Marguerite, was Clytemnestra.

Louis de Troyes stared at the donkey. "I, uh, I'll ask...."

THE *TIRAILLEURS* who had taken refuge in that French farmhouse observed that the storm was over. They thanked their host and hostess, saddled their horses and departed.

With the aid of their telescope, they scanned the beach, first one way and then the other. At first, in the darkness, they could see nothing. Then, they spotted a group of figures by the statue of Sainte Marguerite.

"Smugglers," said one of the group knowingly.

"Or our escaped English!" cried their officer. "After them! Quick! Before they get away! You!" he commanded one of his subordinates. "Ride back and inform Governor Ollivier!"

CLYTEMNESTRA PROVED obstinate. She objected to being dragged away from the fine fodder by the statue of Sainte Marguerite. She dug her heels in and brayed loudly when Lord Brandford suggested she should step onto the raft. She would not swim to the *Venus*, and when they tried to put her in the longboat, she laid her ears back and threatened to kick the bottom out of it.

Worse still, since Lord Brandford had no more comfits to give her, Clytemnestra was now hardly on speaking terms with him. He sighed exasperatedly. Never had he seen an animal so contrary!

MEANWHILE, GOVERNOR Ollivier and his four detachments of *tirailleurs* were now united in one large body of cavalry.

LORD BRANDFORD SAT DOWN with his chin on his hands. A short distance away, Clytemnestra, head lowered, was glaring defiantly at him. He wondered how on earth he was to persuade her to come aboard the *Venus*?

Suddenly, the sound of horses' hooves, muffled by sand, intruded into the peace of the night. Lord Brandford leapt to his feet. "The French!"

The *tirailleurs* were firing even before they had a chance of striking their targets. With their sabres unsheathed, they were bearing down on the longboat and the raft with all the ferocity at their command.

In a trice, Clytemnestra realized the danger she was in, and in the same instant, she decided that perhaps going to England aboard the *Venus* was not such a bad idea as it had seemed at first. Meekly, she submitted to being put aboard the raft and held in place by four hefty seamen, and the longboats took to the water, towing the raft behind them.

The *tirailleurs* charged after them, splashing into the waves and firing wildly. The sailors in the longboats pulled as hard as they were able. Fear gave them strength, and soon they were out of the shallows. They arrived at the port side of the *Venus* without a scratch. For safety's sake, they took the raft to the starboard side where the French guns would not reach. Then they hauled Clytemnestra up, before climbing on deck themselves.

"Anchors aweigh!" shouted the boatswain as the *Venus* turned towards England.

The *tirailleurs*, dripping wet, disappointed and angry, wheeled their horses back onto the beach. They could do nothing now except watch while the yacht, with her sails unfurled, sped away from them.

LORD BRANDFORD LEANED OVER the taffrail, staring at the moonlit water.

Louis de Troyes joined him. "Charles, may I ask you something?"

"Yes, of course."

"What made you bring the donkey?"

"I, er, I promised Emma."

"Ah!" Louis de Troyes surveyed his future brother-in-law. There was an expression on the earl's face which he had never thought he would see there. It was sheepishness.

CHAPTER NINETEEN

"WHAT A GLORIOUS DAY!" exclaimed Lady Brandford as her maid pulled aside the curtains. "It makes one glad to be alive!"

"Yes, my lady," the servant replied, bringing a shawl over to her. "It's quite cool even though the sun is shining."

"Thank you, Nancy." As Lady Brandford descended the plum carpeted staircase to the breakfast room, her heart was light. She was feeling especially cheerful, for her maid had awakened her with the news that her errant son had returned at last.

LORD BRANDFORD'S HOMECOMING had been delayed. There were so many things to be seen to: Xavier Roos, his wife and son had to be settled and found work; Aristide Gouleau now reunited with his brother, Yves, had to be repatriated.

Then there were the seemingly endless official meetings Lord Druce had to report on his mission to the Prince Regent. Several important personages were interested in the details of the escape, and Lord Druce, Louis de Troyes and Lord Brandford had been detained by them. But all that, thank goodness, was over now.

Lady Brandford seated herself at the elegant circular table and ordered a large pot of tea, arranging her diaphanous aquamarine negligee about her. "You had better ask Cook to grill some lamb chops and a couple of sausages Lord Brandford may be hungry." She was quite certain that the earl had not had a bite to eat since he had left for France.

"Very good, my lady," answered Wooster.

"And we shall have some marmalade. The best marmalade, fresh rolls, strawberry jam." Lady Brandford paused to consider. "And I should like some buttered eggs, if you please."

Wooster departed to see that her orders were carried out.

LADY BRANDFORD LAID ASIDE the *Morning Chronicle*. A pot of tea was at her right hand. Buttered eggs had been placed before her, along with strawberry jam, new-baked hot rolls and marmalade. The chops, sausage and other hot food were upon the sideboard.

No one had entered the sunlit breakfast room while she had been lost in concentration upon the state of affairs in Europe. She grimaced. She did not like to eat alone.

"Wooster?" she enquired.

"My lady?" Wooster bowed.

"Where is Lady Marcella?"

"Lady Marcella, my lady, received a message very early this morning, from Miss Lavinia Smythe. Lady Marcella took a carriage directly there. She left word that she would breakfast with Miss Lavinia Smythe."

"Ah!" Lady Brandford cast her eyes over the mantelpiece. "Is that letter there in the gilt-edged envelope from her?"

Wooster studied the envelope referred to. "It is, my lady." He placed it upon a silver tray and presented it to her ladyship.

Lady Brandford slit it open, propped it up against the teapot and read it.

Mother dear,

Have you heard the wonderful news? Charles is back. So is John. And my darling Louis. And everyone is all right!

I am so happy! I never thought I could be so happy! Louis and I have settled the date for our wedding. I can hardly wait until the banns have been called!

"Lavinia sent word just this morning to say that John has proposed to her. He did it so romantically— on one knee at four o'clock in the morning while she was still half asleep and none of the servants were up except her maid, who let him in.

Lady Brandford winced. I really must do something about Marcella's punctuation! she thought. And her syntax! Really! And it is not as though grammar was neglected in her school curriculum!

She read on.

Lavinia would very much like a double wedding, if we wouldn't mind. I think it is a marvellous idea, don't you? I am going to discuss the details with her today. Forgive me for rushing off like this,

Your loving
Marcella

Lady Brandford smiled indulgently.

"How very nice." She folded the letter. "We are to have a double wedding, Wooster. Miss Lavinia Smythe to Lord Druce, and Lady Marcella to Mr. de Troyes."

"Excellent news, my lady," commented the butler.

Lady Brandford sipped her tea. When she finished her buttered eggs she made a sign to Wooster. A footman removed the plate and all the servants, except the butler, departed.

"I believe Lord Druce is staying with us," remarked Lady Brandford.

"He is," confirmed Wooster.

"Where did you put him, by the way?"

"Lord Druce is sleeping in the green room, my lady." On receiving a look of encouragement, he added, "He came in with Lord Brandford, but he went out again a little later. He returned only at about six."

Lady Brandford nodded. "He ought not to be wakened."

"No, my lady."

"And Mr. de Troyes?"

"He is in the blue room, my lady. He also returned with Lord Brandford. He and Lady Marcella spoke for about an hour, then each retired for the night."

"I see. Let me know when Mr. de Troyes comes down, please, Wooster."

"Very good, my lady."

Lady Brandford smiled to herself. A double wedding! she mused. Nothing could be more pleasing than a double wedding—unless, of course, it is a triple wedding!

She considered the matter. Emma had left London—foolish child. But Lady Brandford knew that the earl would soon bring her back and then, perhaps, reflected her ladyship, she might look forward to a triple wedding. It would mean, however, persuading both her son and future daughter-in-law, so the sooner she started, Lady Brandford decided, the better.

"Where is Lord Brandford?" she enquired.

"Lord Brandford is asleep in his own room, my lady," Wooster informed her. Then, in a voice of impending doom, he warned, "And there is a donkey in the Conservatory."

CHAPTER TWENTY

LADY BRANDFORD'S EQUILIBRIUM deserted her. The knife
fell from her nerveless fingers onto her plate as she stared
distractedly at the butler.

"A donkey? In the Conservatory?"

Wooster reaffirmed the disquieting news. "Yes, my lady."

Lady Brandford's bread and jam lay untouched in front
of her. "H-how...?" she choked out.

"When his lordship returned home last night, he brought
with him a donkey, which he had placed in the Conservatory. It has a white face. Its coat is grey. Upon its shoulders
are the markings of a cross, said to be common to donkeys
since Our Lord rode upon one on Palm Sunday. Its name is
Clytemnestra."

Lady Brandford blinked. She had had a classical educa-
tion. She had learned about the ancient Greeks: their cul-
ture; their mythology; their legends. The name Clytemnestra
stuck in her memory. Clytemnestra was a queen. She had,
with the connivance of her lover, murdered her husband,
King Agamemnon. And here was this donkey, also called
Clytemnestra, who was now murdering her ladyship's
plants.

"Really?" Lady Brandford's restraint was admirable.
"Perhaps you would be so good as to see if Lord Brandford is awake yet, and if he is, to ask him to join me here for
breakfast. At once."

"Yes, my lady. Very good, my lady." With these words,
Wooster withdrew.

Lady Brandford looked at the bronze carriage clock on the sideboard between the lamb chops and the sausages. She picked up her knife, plucked a piece of bread from her roll and spread it with butter and jam. But her movements were mechanical, for she was no longer hungry. But one had to keep up appearances, even in this most dreadful crisis.

Less than five minutes elapsed before the doors of the breakfast room were opened and a dishevelled Earl of Brandford entered, suppressing a yawn. Wooster, who was behind him, closed the silvered doors.

"Good morning, Mother dear." Lord Brandford kissed her cheek.

"You haven't shaved!" rebuked Lady Brandford.

"You wanted to see me *at once*, Mother dear. There wasn't time to shave." Lord Brandford adjusted the folds of his chocolate-brown dressing gown and seated himself in his usual chair, looking hopefully at the teapot.

Lady Brandford poured. The tea was dark and very strong. She passed a cup to her son. "Would you have a fresh pot made, please, Wooster."

Wooster bowed. "Will there be anything else?"

"Yes. Just before you go, Wooster..." Unconsciously, she rearranged the greying curls which peeped out from under her lace-trimmed mobcap. "Charles, Wooster informs me that there is a donkey in the Conservatory."

The Earl of Brandford's brown eyes widened with surprise. "What? Only one?"

Lady Brandford stared at her son, appalled. Somehow, she managed to whisper, "Wh-what do you m-mean—*only one!*"

"I distinctly remember purchasing a second donkey."

Lady Brandford choked.

"I thought Clytemnestra—the original donkey—might be lonely," continued Lord Brandford. "So I purchased Nobs. Nobs is a stallion, and Clytemnestra is a mare, so they should get on famously." He addressed the butler. "Perhaps when you bring the tea, Wooster, you would also ascertain if Nobs has arrived?"

Wooster's face, as he bowed himself out, was a picture. One donkey was bad enough—but two! If it ever became known.... Wooster dared not contemplate such a catastrophe. He shivered at the mere thought of it. For a gentleman to breed horses was one thing. For a gentleman to breed donkeys—quite another! And that he, Wooster, most impeccable of butlers, should serve an earl who kept a stable of...donkeys! *I shall be a laughing stock!* reflected Wooster in horror.

By the time he reached the kitchen, he was trembling. He had served the Earls of Brandford for twenty years. No one had been able to entice him away, though many had tried. Yet now, for the first time in his life, Wooster was seriously considering giving notice!

LADY BRANDFORD LOOKED accusingly at her son. "When your father gave me that Conservatory," she observed in wounded tones, "it was so that I could grow my beloved plants. I have a mulberry tree, the finest vine outside Hampton Court Palace, an orange tree that I grew from a pip, and flowers..." Tearfully, she continued, "Adam and Eve themselves would have envied me my flowers." Her eyes flashed. "Your father did *not* give me all that so that my efforts could be munched to a pulp by a herd of donkeys!"

Lord Brandford was blandly innocent. "Only two donkeys, Mother dear."

"They will still eat up everything in sight!"

"Goats, Mother dear."

"I beg your pardon?"

"It is goats who eat everything in sight." Having finished his tea, he rose and lifted one of the covers upon the sideboard. "Ah! Lamb chops! Excellent!" He helped himself to three. "You needn't worry about your plants. Donkeys are far more fastidious than goats."

Lady Brandford was totally sceptical.

Lord Brandford sat down again and dug into his chops. "Of course, there are exceptions, but Clytemnestra and Nobs are, er, housetrained. As far as I have been able to tell, they have shown no interest in the things in your Conservatory."

"There is always a first time!" muttered Lady Brandford darkly.

Wooster returned, bearing a pot of fresh tea and a jug of hot water, which he deposited at Lady Brandford's right hand. He straightened.

"I beg to inform your lordship that there are now two donkeys in the Conservatory—"

"Good!" exclaimed Lord Brandford, ignoring his mother's devastating gaze.

"—and a disreputable character."

"Ah! That will be their handler. Be so good as to see if he has had breakfast."

"Very good, my lord."

"Oh, and Wooster—"

"Yes, my lord."

"Does he speak French?"

Wooster looked as if the rug had been whipped out from underneath him. "I—I have no idea . . . my lord."

"Ah! Pity. Never mind. I am sure I shall find out eventually."

"Er, yes, my lord." When Wooster retired, his brow was covered—most unusually for him—in perspiration.

WHEN THEY WERE ALONE once more, Lady Brandford stirred the tea, left the leaves to settle and poured. "French? You want a donkey handler who speaks French?"

"Clytemnestra is a French donkey. Her original owners were Greek—hence the name. But she is a French donkey and I assumed that she would understand French better than English. I particularly asked for a donkey handler who spoke French and English."

Lady Brandford placed her slender hand upon the plush bell rope and rang.

Wooster reappeared.

"Wooster, would you be so good as to bring me the decanter of whiskey?"

Wooster bowed and departed, then returned with the crystal decanter and placed it before her ladyship. His voice, when he managed to find it, was ragged. "I am informed by the staff...my lord...that the donkey handler does, indeed...speak French. And—" Wooster coughed "—that he has consumed half a loaf of bread and butter, a kippered herring and some jam."

"Excellent. Thank you, Wooster," responded the earl.

Wooster, pale as death, retreated.

"WHY," DEMANDED Lady Brandford, as soon as Wooster had gone, "in the name of heaven, Charles, did you get a donkey who spoke French?"

"I didn't. Emma did."

Lady Brandford laced her tea with whiskey and swallowed it in one gulp. "Emma?" she squeaked.

"Yes, Emma. She bought the donkey and used it to help the men escape. Clytemnestra was invaluable. Emma felt she did not want to leave the animal in French hands so I—" Lord Brandford blushed "—I brought her back with us."

Lady Brandford abandoned all pretense of drinking tea. She filled her flower-patterned teacup with whiskey and drank the spirit neat.

"Charles," she said in strangled tones, "are you seriously going to sit there and tell me that when you...when you were in mortal danger... *you actually arranged for a donkey to be shipped to Dover?*"

"Yes, Mother dear." Lord Brandford, seeing the stopper of the decanter lying upon the delicately embroidered linen tablecloth, replaced it. "There was no other way."

Lady Brandford fanned herself vigorously with the *Morning Chronicle*. "Charles, you cannot...you surely do not intend to keep the donkeys...in the Conservatory?"

"Of course not, Mother dear," answered Lord Brandford complacently. "I shall take them to the Houghton Academy for Young Ladies and present them to Miss Foxall and Miss Quince." He looked suddenly suspicious. "That is where Emma has gone, isn't it?"

Lady Brandford nodded, as relief flooded over her.

"Thank goodness!" murmured Lord Brandford. "I was afraid for one awful moment she had gone on another rescue mission to the Continent. I couldn't bear it!"

"Ah!" Lady Brandford actually found the strength to smile again. She refilled her teacup, this time with tea. "You do mean to marry Emma, don't you?"

"Of course."

Lady Brandford put her head on one side. "You know that I have given Marcella permission to marry Louis?"

"Yes. He told me." Lord Brandford seemed quite unconcerned.

Lady Brandford pursed her lips. "You are eating too fast, Charles. You will ruin your digestion. You ought to chew every mouthful a hundred—"

"I haven't time for that."

His mother glanced at him in query.

"As soon as I have finished breakfast, I shall dress and go to Houghton Regina."

"Oh."

"The donkeys are to be sent on ahead."

"I see." The world was a beautiful place once more. The birds were singing, the sun was shining, and...there was the prospect of a triple wedding. Lady Brandford decided to introduce the subject. "John has proposed to Lavinia..." she began.

"Good." The earl did not look up.

"They are going to marry."

"Wonderful."

"It will be a double wedding. Marcella and Louis; Lavinia and John."

"Perfect." He could hardly have seemed less interested.

"You wouldn't care to make it a triple wedding, would you?" Their eyes met. Lady Brandford appealed silently to her son.

"When is this double wedding?" enquired her son, cautiously.

"In just four weeks. We can have the banns called..."

"I can't wait that long."

"That long! But it is hardly any time at all!"

"Mother dear, it is imperative that I propose to Emma and marry her before she comes up with another bright idea. As her husband, I can prevent her more dangerous and harebrained schemes. As a mere friend, I wouldn't stand a chance."

Lady Brandford's fingers were interlaced. "You mightn't be able to stop her if you were her husband, either."

"Perhaps not, but at least I can see to it that she makes sensible arrangements and doesn't run off half-cocked—"

"Really, Charles! Where do you find these vulgar expressions?"

Lord Brandford, his mouth full of bread and marmalade, did not reply. His plate was almost clear. He stood up. "Excuse me, Mother dear," he mumbled.

Lady Brandford sighed exasperatedly as he made for the door.

"A triple wedding would be so nice," she observed cunningly. "I am sure Emma would—"

"No!" Lord Brandford cut her short.

His forcefulness took her aback. Forgetting that he was fifteen feet away from her, she cowered in her chair.

"I love you very much, Mother dear," continued her son, "but I am not going to accede to this notion of a triple wedding. Emma and I shall be married the moment I reach Houghton Regina. I have the necessary licence in my pocket."

Lady Brandford opened her mouth to protest.

"And that," added her son, "is final."

CHAPTER TWENTY-ONE

MISS QUINCE WAS REVIEWING the assessments of the pupils at the Houghton Academy for Young Ladies, which had been made by the staff. Miss Foxall was by her side, making judicious comments.

The June day was a peaceful and quiet one: here and there a girl's voice floated up to them from the garden, a bird perched upon a branch of the chestnut tree, a gentle breeze rustled the privet hedge, and down the lane, a dog barked.

All at once it seemed that there was an orchestra of shouts and whoops of delight. A gaggle of girls was in a state of undue excitement.

Miss Quince raised her head. "What is that noise, Artemisia?"

Miss Foxall stood up. She smoothed the folds of her poppy-painted muslin gown. "It does not sound like a fight." Striding to the open window, she peered out. Then her steely eyebrows arched, and her spectacles descended from her nose to her bosom, where they hung, suspended upon their black velvet ribbons. "Donkeys!"

"Donkeys?"

"The girls are crowding around a pair of grey, long-eared quadrupeds, known to the Romans as *asinus*, masculine, and *asina*, feminine. In the vernacular, they are, I believe, commonly called donkeys."

Miss Quince got up and came to the window. Below, on the front lawn, she could see half the pupils of the Academy. And two donkeys.

One donkey had a straw hat upon its head; the other was decked with a garland of flowers. A swarthy man in garish attire—certainly *not* a gentleman—was holding on to the donkeys' bridles.

The girls were cooing ecstatically.

"Oh, aren't they lovely?"

"Aren't they delightful?"

"Don't they have beautiful faces?"

"May I give them a carrot?"

"Do they like sugar?"

"May we ride them?"

Miss Foxall and Miss Quince exchanged glances.

"Emma!" intoned Miss Foxall.

Miss Quince uttered a cry of alarm. "Oh, no! Emma wouldn't! She knows better than to try and turn our Academy into a—a fairground!"

"Harrmph!" snorted Miss Foxall, certain that Emma was behind it. Perhaps not intentionally, but there was—mercifully—only one pupil at the Academy who could possibly have conjured up donkeys!

"I shall speak to her," threatened Miss Foxall. "Severely!"

"Now, now, Artemisia," soothed Miss Quince. "Let us not be hasty...."

At that moment, the wrought-iron gates of the Houghton Academy for Young Ladies admitted a glossy, black-lacquered carriage. Miss Quince's far-sighted gaze took note of the arms emblazoned upon the doors. She sighed. "I am very much afraid, Artemisia, my dear, that you are right. At least in principle. The Earl of Brandford has just arrived. It cannot be coincidence."

LORD BRANDFORD WAS USHERED into the drawing room. The doors were closed behind him, shutting out the eager, curious gazes of the younger members of the Academy.

There, he faced the united front of Miss Foxall and Miss Quince, who welcomed him with reserve and a hint of disapproval.

"Lord Brandford," commenced Miss Foxall, "we are naturally delighted to see that you are safely returned from France."

"Thank you."

"However, there is a matter we would like to discuss with you...."

"The donkeys," completed Miss Quince.

Lord Brandford smiled. "The female is Clytemnestra. The male is Nobs. Their handler is an excellent fellow, who fully understands the need for discretion."

Miss Foxall and Miss Quince lowered themselves into the cream-upholstered, straight-backed chairs. With a gesture, they invited Lord Brandford to take the third.

"Are we to understand," ventured Miss Quince, "that the donkeys are..."

"A gift," said the Earl of Brandford. "From Miss Armstead and myself."

"I knew Emma was at the bottom of this!" muttered Miss Foxall.

"I beg your pardon?"

"That is extremely generous of you, Lord Brandford," amended Miss Foxall. "And of Miss Armstead, too. But—"

"Oh, I see. The young ladies are not yet used to the novelty of them." The Earl of Brandford smiled winningly. "I assure you it will soon wear off."

Miss Quince brushed a speck of fluff from her amber-and-pearl striped gown.

"Donkeys are so useful, you see," proceeded Lord Brandford, "for young ladies of a delicate constitution. And for those who cannot ride horses. My sister became very fond of them when she was younger. She had consumption and rode donkeys on the beach. She is quite recovered now.''

Miss Foxall and Miss Quince exchanged glances.

"Are we to understand, Lord Brandford,'' enquired Miss Foxall, ''that these donkeys will benefit the health of our pupils?''

"The physicians esteem them for such purposes.''

"Ah!''

That was altogether another matter, for the donkeys would thus become *respectable*. There was, however, one more problem. Miss Foxall looked at Miss Quince.

Miss Quince cleared her throat. "Of course, there is the question of the donkey handler...."

"Mr. Noonan Unwin,'' supplied Lord Brandford.

"Ahem! Yes. And Mr. Noonan Unwin's clothes. They are, er, rather loud.''

Lord Brandford smiled. "Of course, Miss Armstead and I shall provide Mr. Unwin with suitable attire—a uniform which he may wear here. We shall also pay his salary, as part of our gift.''

"Too kind,'' murmured both Headmistresses in unison.

"Mr. Unwin is a married man,'' continued Lord Brandford, "blessed with eight children.''

The headmistresses' eyes flew open. Eight children!

"I do hope,'' said Miss Foxall dryly, ''that they are well-behaved.''

"Their parents will see to it that they are,'' stated the earl.

Miss Foxall inclined her head.

"In that case,'' said Miss Quince, "we should be most happy to accept your and Miss Armstead's extremely generous gift.''

Lord Brandford made a gesture of acknowledgement.

Meanwhile, the noise outside had become deafening. "If you don't mind, Lord Brandford,'' remarked Miss Foxall, "we shall leave you here while we attend to the girls and see that they don't altogether lose their heads over the donkeys."

Lord Brandford rose and bowed, as the two Headmistresses marched out to deal with their charges.

They had not been gone more than a couple of seconds, when the drawing room door opened and Emma entered. She folded her hands demurely in front of her. Her eyes were cast downwards.

"I have come to thank you, Lord Brandford," she began formally, "for bringing Clytemnestra here and for providing her with a companion."

She had no chance to say any more. At the sound of her voice, the earl had started towards her. He gathered her in his arms. Their lips met, and all else was forgotten in the sweetness of their kiss.

CHAPTER TWENTY-TWO

"MMMM," MURMURED EMMA ecstatically as they parted. She gazed dreamily at him.

How handsome he is! she thought.

His brown hair, though she had ruffled it, looked fashionably windswept, not unkempt. His azure broadcloth coat enhanced his lean muscular form, just as the grey-and-white-striped marcella waistcoat discreetly complemented his fob. His nankeen breeches fitted without a wrinkle, drawing Emma's attention to his very fine legs.

Then she realized that he was gazing at her and unaccountably, she was overcome with shyness.

"You—you are looking very well, Lord Brandford."

The earl put his hands on his hips and scowled at her. "Emma, how can you possibly call me Lord Brandford when we are going to be married? It will not do! It is too stiff, too formal. I shall not allow it. You called me Charles before you returned here. You can go on calling me Charles—especially when you are my wife!"

Emma swished her pink cambric skirt. "Is that . . . a proposal?"

"Yes."

Emma looked down at her white leather slippers.

"What is the matter?"

"Well . . ." began Emma slowly, "in all that I have heard or read upon the subject, when a man proposes it is usual for him to kneel before his intended and say 'Will you marry me?' or words to that effect. And before that happens, he has to court her, bring her flowers and bonbons...."

Lord Brandford's black eyebrows drew together.

"You have not brought me flowers," accused Emma.

"No."

"Nor bonbons."

"No."

"You did not kneel before me."

"Nor shall I!"

"I beg your pardon?"

"Do you know what would happen if I knelt before you? The inestimable young ladies of this Academy would know it in a trice. They would line up outside the drawing-room window, gawking at us. And they would giggle. I have no intention of making a spectacle of myself for the benefit of a hundred or so giggling schoolgirls!"

Emma smiled. "You have a point."

"Besides," Lord Brandford's voice dropped to a hoarse whisper, as his arms closed about her again, "I have already said I love you. I meant it. I do love you—beyond anything I can put into words, or say with flowers or bonbons. So, will you marry me, Emma? Please? Tomorrow?"

His lips were chasing down Emma's lily-white neck. She revelled in the sensations shooting through her.

"Yes! Oh yes, Charles!" And then, she whispered hesitantly, "I—I do love you...so very much!"

Time was suspended while he kissed her once more, and it was only Clytemnestra's loud braying which made them stop.

They both heaved a sigh of relief as they realized that the donkey was not right at their elbows, but outside, being led to the stables, along with Nobs, Mr. Unwin and the entire Unwin family, and that her braying was merely a demand for yet another piece of sugar.

"I, er, gave Clytemnestra and Nobs to Miss Foxall and Miss Quince." Lord Brandford was still breathless from Emma's kisses. "As a gift. For their pupils…from both of us."

"What a wonderful idea!" Emma managed to gasp, trembling with delight. "So thoughtful. Everyone will love the donkeys. And Clytemnestra will be so happy."

"You didn't want her for yourself?"

Emma shook her head.

"I'm glad."

He seemed to hear his mother's voice adding dryly, "Not as glad as I am, Charles!"

His arms encircled Emma once more. Their lips had scarcely touched when the door opened wide. Miss Foxall and Miss Quince had returned.

Miss Foxall stopped short. "What is the meaning of this, Lord Brandford?"

The earl disengaged himself from Emma. "Miss Armstead and I are to be married."

"Tomorrow," added Emma.

Miss Foxall's and Miss Quince's eyebrows rose simultaneously. They turned their heads towards each other, and the former's dark grey eyes met the latter's light grey ones.

"Don't you think," enquired Miss Foxall, "you should ask our permission first?"

Lord Brandford stiffened. "Your permission?"

"Miss Armstead is not yet of age. As her guardians, it falls to us to give our consent—"

"—Or not, as the case may be," completed Miss Quince.

This obstacle to Lord Brandford's happiness came as a complete surprise. He was speechless.

Miss Foxall took the opportunity to cross to the pea-green tapestried chaise longue and seat herself in one corner. Miss Quince arranged herself decorously in the other corner.

Miss Foxall gazed up. "Do pray be seated, Lord Brand‑
ford. You are towering over us, and it is making me ner‑
vous." She did not sound the least bit nervous.

Lord Brandford, however, having first placed Emma i‑
one of the creamy Sheraton armchairs, dutifully seate‑
himself opposite the two Headmistresses.

Miss Foxall surveyed him through her pince-nez. "Th‑
late Colonel Armstead appointed us his daughter's guard‑
ans."

"Papa did not think it right," interpolated Emma, "tha‑
if anything happened to him, I should be left alone in th‑
world. He wanted someone who would care for me, wh‑
could bring me up properly."

"We were, of course, honoured by his trust in us," sai‑
Miss Quince, "though deeply saddened by his loss and b‑
the subsequent necessity of accepting the responsibility."

"I see." Lord Brandford's sensitive face had darkened‑
"And is there any reason why you should refuse your con‑
sent to our union?"

Miss Foxall and Miss Quince studied the couple. Onc‑
more, they exchanged glances.

"You won't stop us from marrying, will you?" aske‑
Emma eagerly. "We are so absolutely right for each othe‑
You can't possibly say no!"

"You know what will happen if we say no," muttere‑
Miss Quince to Miss Foxall.

"An elopement?"

Miss Quince nodded.

Miss Foxall raised her eyes to the heavens. "Thes‑
impetuous youngsters of today!" she murmured. "When w‑
were young, people were content to wait. Patiently." Then‑
more firmly, she remarked, "Tomorrow, Lord Brandford‑
is rather *soon*."

Lord Brandford drummed his fingers on his knee. "‑
don't see why."

"There are certain formalities to be settled."

Lord Brandford scowled at her. "What formalities?"

"The late Colonel Armstead left a marriage contract...."

Lord Brandford shrugged negligently. "Well, bring it here and we'll sign it and have done with it."

"You take the matter extraordinarily lightly," commented Miss Quince.

"I don't consider it important."

"Even though by the terms of it, you may not touch a penny of Miss Armstead's fortune?"

Lord Brandford stared in amazement. "Her... what?"

"My fortune." Emma tossed her head, making her golden curls dance.

"You are... an heiress?"

"Yes. Didn't you know?"

Lord Brandford, dazed, shook his head. "I had no idea."

"You did not surely imagine Miss Armstead was a pauper?" challenged Miss Foxall.

"I did not think about it at all." His lips curved into a smile. "It doesn't make any difference, one way or the other. I love her, you see."

Emma's heart sang. *I have my wish*, she thought joyfully. She was loved for herself alone: her fortune did not matter.

"How soon can you have the contract here?" the earl was asking.

"By this evening," replied Miss Foxall.

"Good. Then we can still be married tomorrow—"

"Without a wedding dress?" demanded Miss Quince, scandalized.

"Miss Armstead must have something suitable to wear!" agreed Miss Foxall.

"Oh, but I have!" exclaimed Emma.

"I beg your pardon?"

"Ever since I returned from the Continent," responded Emma, "my friends have been sewing me a wedding dress.

Miss Young supervised the work, of course.'' Miss Youn
taught needlework. "The dress is quite finished."

"In that case," declared Miss Quince, "we see no fur
ther impediments to your union. We shall send for ou
solicitors at once regarding the marriage contract. I tru:
you will make the other arrangements, Lord Brandford?'

The earl bowed.

Miss Foxall and Miss Quince inclined their heads. The
they rose, linked arms and made a regal exit from the draw
ing room. As soon as they were alone in the hall, Miss Fo;
all turned to Miss Quince.

"I knew," she confided, "there was something behind th
girls' sudden enthusiasm for their needlework!"

LORD BRANDFORD EYED his beloved quizzically. "Were yo
so very sure of me?"

Emma's blush was the same shade of pink as her dres;
Her eyes dropped, and she shuffled her foot. "I wasn't sur
of you at all."

"But the wedding dress! You have it ready!"

"Ah! That was my friends' doing, you see."

"No, I don't see."

Emma, still refusing to meet his passionate gaze, a;
swered, "When I came back, I told my best friend, Kath
erine Verrier, about you. She said, 'Well, if he's like tha
he'll probably come up here and demand that you be ma
ried tomorrow, and what on earth are you going to wear?'
said you wouldn't do it that way at all. It would be a
ranged properly, with Lady Brandford taking a hand in i
I intimated it would take at least six months."

"So it would have if I had let her!"

"Anyway, Susanna Thirske said, 'You might as well hav
a dress just in case,' though I pointed out to her and to tl
others that you might not be going to propose to me at all.'

Lord Brandford groaned. "How could you think such
thing after what passed between us in Belgium?"

Emma twisted her hands this way and that, and her cheeks were still bright pink. With her eyes still cast down, she did not notice that he had come closer. "You might simply have sent me Clytemnestra."

"No. Never." One hand lazily tweaked her golden curls.

Emma's heart was pounding. "So you say—now. But I wasn't sure...." She paused. "However, my friends wouldn't listen. I told them it would be dreadful if I had a wedding dress and no proposal. So Pamela Irish suggested we shouldn't tell anyone...."

He was nibbling her ear. It made it very difficult to concentrate.

"Pamela said we should ask Miss Young if we might make a wedding dress as a test of our skill in needlework. Of course, Miss Young agreed, and since I am older than the others, it was suggested that I should be the model. That way my friends knew—and they were sworn to secrecy—but the teachers didn't. Thus, if you didn't propose, I wouldn't be a laughingstock."

His kisses trailed in a line down her milk-white throat.

"So there you are!" she declared defiantly. "I was bullied into it."

"Yes. I see." Lord Brandford's lips closed over hers.

"Besides—" Emma was nearly breathless from his kisses "—if I hadn't had the dress...to occupy me, I should have...gone mad with worry."

He straightened at once. "But you knew I was all right!"

"I didn't dare to believe it until I saw you here."

He silenced her with more of those devastating kisses.

"You...understand?"

"I understand. But do you realize, my darling, what it means?"

"It means I shall have something to wear."

"It means we shall not be having the small quiet wedding I had planned, since the entire school will have to be invited."

IT WAS ONLY LATER, when Emma saw the Special Licence, that it occurred to her to ask, in her turn, "Were *you* that sure of *me*?"

The Earl of Brandford started. "Sure of you?"

"The Special Licence..." she began.

A dark flush spread over his lean countenance. "I wasn't sure of you at all." He laughed self-deprecatingly. "You are the most unpredictable woman I have ever met! I simply knew that if you said yes, I could not endure a long engagement."

Emma put her head on one side. "And if I had chanced to say no?"

"I don't dare to contemplate what I would have done!"

THE CHURCH OF ST. ETHELBURGA the Virgin, in Houghton Regina, was packed to overflowing. Every now and then, excited young ladies began chattering—or worse, indulging in their mirth. From his ornate, oak pulpit, carved in the manner of Grinling Gibbons, Canon Jupper fixed them with a beady eye.

"Hush!" hissed their teachers, and a temporary silence ensued. Then the talking and the laughing started again.

The Earl of Brandford, exquisitely attired in a navy-blue silk coat, stood stalwartly by the gilded altar and contrived to ignore the young ladies.

Miss Foxall and Miss Quince had tendered him that advice, with the warning that if he were to pay them undue attention at such a time, it would only spur them on.

Miss Quince had put on her best white muslin gown with a heliotrope bonnet and shawl to match. She gazed reflectively at the earl. After several moments' pensive thought she addressed Miss Foxall, "Artemisia, shall Emma, in your opinion, be able to manage him?"

Miss Foxall glanced from his lordship to his bride. Emma Armstead was wearing a delicate Honiton-lace veil that altogether hid her face. Her wedding dress was of white gauze neatly embroidered with silver lilies of the valley and finished with a scalloped border.

"I really believe, Naomi my dear, that question should have been put the other way round. Is *he* going to be able to manage Emma?"

"What do you mean?"

"From the way he is looking at her now, there is a great danger she will wrap him rather too well around her little finger."

"Oh, dear! I do hope he is firm and puts his foot down with her—at least occasionally."

"Yes. She needs that."

The two Headmistresses contemplated the happy couple for several seconds, then Miss Foxall adjusted her pince-nez.

"Naomi, I am persuaded he will curb Emma's wilder schemes."

"I am glad you think he has that much sense. A young man in love can be..."

"Ah, yes!" agreed Miss Foxall. "I remember how it was!"

SUMMER WAS ALMOST OVER. The Houghton Academy for Young Ladies was an oasis of tranquillity, for the pupils had not yet returned from their holidays, and the teachers were only just beginning to make plans for the new term.

Miss Foxall passed Miss Quince a cup of tea.

"Thank you, my dear," said Miss Quince. She took a sip. "I needed that."

"The accounts?" queried Miss Foxall sympathetically.

"Yes." Miss Quince had totalled the list of expenses, and entered the sum in the marbled volume before her.

"How are we faring?"

"Very well!"

"Better than last year?"

"Decidedly."

"To what do we owe that, do you suppose?"

"Donkeys."

"I beg your pardon?"

"The donkeys which Lord Brandford and Emma Armstead, as she was then, gave us. They are a great success. The girls love them."

"Yes. The girls would. They are altogether overly fond of whatsoever may get them into mischief!"

Miss Quince laughed. "But Artemisia, their parents and guardians consider that the donkeys are an excellent idea, too."

"You astonish me!" Miss Foxall reclined upon the sofa and stirred up a breeze with a parchment fan adorned with a portrait of the Prince Regent.

"Indeed? Let me assure you, Artemisia, that the donkeys are highly esteemed. So much better for young ladies than horses for riding!"

"If you mean that the girls are less likely to break their necks if they fall off, then I agree."

"Their parents and guardians feel, as Lord Brandford does, that the donkeys are conducive to good health. The Academy has improved in standing wonderfully since their arrival. We have received many more applications for places. We may even need another couple of teachers."

"Really? Two more teachers? That is encouraging!" Miss Foxall paused for thought. "And," she added impishly, "another pair of donkeys?"

Miss Quince surveyed her venerable colleague. "We shall consider it when we have sorted out the teachers' salaries."

IT WAS A VERY HOT AUGUST DAY. Lady Brandford had been to the Pump Rooms in Bath to take the waters, and their metallic flavour lingered in her mouth. She grimaced.

Her carriage continued at its sedate pace until it arrived at Brandford Hall. Lady Brandford descended, glancing behind her, as she always did, for a view of Bath in the distance.

Lady Marcella, jumping up and down with excitement, met her on the front porch. "Mother dear! They're back!"

"Do you mean Emma and Charles?"

"Yes, she does," replied Louis de Troyes, placing an arm possessively about his wife's shoulder. "They are inside, changing."

Lady Brandford glided into the spacious vestibule. The first person who met her gaze was the new Lady Druce. "Lavinia my dear! How good to see you. I do hope Marcella and Louis have been making you welcome."

"Very welcome, indeed," answered Lord Druce, emerging from the library. He kissed Lady Brandford's hand. "Have you heard? Charles is back—with Emma."

Even as he spoke, Lord Brandford, now in a coffee-coloured cloth coat, left his dressing room. Together with Emma, he walked to the top of the stairs.

Emma put her hand on the broad, well-polished bannister. A speculative gleam shone in her blue eyes.

"No!" whispered the earl.

Emma grinned at him. "Not even once?"

"No!"

"They are very nice bannisters for sliding down...."

His hand tightened on her arm. "I beg to differ."

Emma sighed. "Perhaps you are right."

She allowed him to lead her down the stairs.

Lady Brandford met them as they reached the bottom, and enveloped Emma in an affectionate embrace, exclaiming, "You are looking wonderful, my dear. Marriage agrees with you."

"Thank you, Mother dear."

Lady Brandford offered her cheek to her son. "Charles, I really must remonstrate with you. A honeymoon is supposed to take two *weeks*, not two *months!*"

The Earl of Brandford kissed his mother. "Really, Mother dear? You amaze me. Emma, did you know that?"

Emma was innocence itself. "No. But then I have not been married before. I daresay I shall know more about these matters when I have had some practice."

At this, Lady Brandford seemed too bewildered to speak.

Louis de Troyes ended the awkwardness. "You have not heard the details of our double wedding yet."

"Oh, yes!" exclaimed Lavinia. "We must tell you! Such dresses! So many guests! And the service..."

THE SUN HAD SET. Emma was wearing a cotton nightgown, as it was far too warm for anything else. She stood by the open window, gazing up at the stars twinkling in the night sky.

Behind her, the floor creaked. Lord Brandford was advancing towards her in the darkness.

"Louis and Marcella looked so very happy," murmured Emma. "So did Lavinia and John."

His hands rested lightly on her shoulders. "But not as happy as you and I, my love."

Emma favoured him with a brilliant smile. Her hands came up to draw his head down, and as her lips brushed his, she felt a tremor of passion shaking him. Then suddenly he gathered her in his arms and carried her sure-footedly across the room to their bed....

Take 4 bestselling love stories FREE

Plus get a FREE surprise gift!

PASSPORT TO ROMANCE
SWEEPSTAKES RULES

1. **HOW TO ENTER:** To enter, you must be the age of majority and complete the official entry form, or print your name address, telephone number and age on a plain piece of paper and mail to Passport to Romance, P.O Box 9056, Buffalo, NY 14269-9056. No mechanically reproduced entries accepted.

2. All entries must be received by the CONTEST CLOSING DATE, DECEMBER 31, 1990 TO BE ELIGIBLE.

3. **THE PRIZES:** There will be ten (10) Grand Prizes awarded, each consisting of a choice of a trip for two people from the following list·
   i) London, England (approximate retail value $5,050 U.S.)
   ii) England, Wales and Scotland (approximate retail value $6,400 U.S.)
   iii) Carribean Cruise (approximate retail value $7,300 U.S.)
   iv) Hawaii (approximate retail value $9,550 U.S.)
   v) Greek Island Cruise in the Mediterranean (approximate retail value $12,250 U.S.)
   vi) France (approximate retail value $7,300 U.S.)

4. Any winner may choose to receive any trip or a cash alternative prize of $5,000.00 U.S. in lieu of the trip.

5. **GENERAL RULES:** Odds of winning depend on number of entries received.

6. A random draw will be made by Nielsen Promotion Services, an independent judging organization, on January 29, 1991, in Buffalo, NY, at 11.30 a.m. from all eligible entries received on or before the Contest Closing Date.

7. Any Canadian entrants who are selected must correctly answer a time-limited, mathematical skill-testing question in order to win.

8. Full contest rules may be obtained by sending a stamped, self-addressed envelope to: "Passport to Romance Rules Request", P.O Box 9998, Saint John, New Brunswick, Canada E2L 4N4.

9. Quebec residents may submit any litigation respecting the conduct and awarding of a prize in this contest to the Régie des loteries et courses du Québec.

10. Payment of taxes other than air and hotel taxes is the sole responsibility of the winner.

11. Void where prohibited by law

COUPON BOOKLET OFFER TERMS

To receive your Free travel-savings coupon booklets, complete the mail-in Offer Certificate on the preceeding page, including the necessary number of proofs-of-purchase, and mail to: Passport to Romance, P.O Box 9057, Buffalo, NY 14269-9057 The coupon booklets include savings on travel-related products such as car rentals, hotels, cruises, flowers and restaurants. Some restrictions apply The offer is available in the United States and Canada. Requests must be postmarked by January 25, 1991 Only proofs-of-purchase from specially marked "Passport to Romance" Harlequin® or Silhouette® books will be accepted. The offer certificate must accompany your request and may not be reproduced in any manner. Offer void where prohibited or restricted by law LIMIT FOUR COUPON BOOKLETS PER NAME, FAMILY, GROUP, ORGANIZATION OR ADDRESS. Please allow up to 8 weeks after receipt of order for shipment. Enter quickly as quantities are limited Unfulfilled mail-in offer requests will receive free Harlequin® or Silhouette® books (not previously available in retail stores), in quantities equal to the number of proofs-of-purchase required for Levels One to Four, as applicable.

OFFICIAL SWEEPSTAKES
ENTRY FORM

Complete and return this Entry Form immediately—the more Entry Forms you submit, the better your chances of winning!
- Entry Forms must be received by **December 31, 1990**
- A random draw will take place on **January 29, 1991**
- Trip must be taken by **December 31, 1991**

3-HRG-3-SW

YES, I want to win a PASSPORT TO ROMANCE vacation for two! I understand the prize includes round-trip air fare, accommodation and a daily spending allowance.

Name_____

Address_____

City_____ State_____ Zip_____

Telephone Number_____ Age_____

Return entries to: **PASSPORT TO ROMANCE**, P.O. Box 9056, Buffalo, NY 14269-9056

© 1990 Harlequin Enterprises Limited

COUPON BOOKLET/OFFER CERTIFICATE

Item	LEVEL ONE Booklet 1	LEVEL TWO Booklet 1 & 2	LEVEL THREE Booklet 1, 2 & 3	LEVEL FOUR Booklet 1, 2, 3 & 4
Booklet 1 = $100+	$100+	$100+	$100+	$100+
Booklet 2 = $200+		$200+	$200+	$200+
Booklet 3 = $300+			$300+	$300+
Booklet 4 = $400+	____	____	____	$400+
Approximate Total Value of Savings	$100+	$300+	$600+	$1,000+
# of Proofs of Purchase Required	4	6	12	18
Check One	____	____	____	____

Name_____

Address_____

City_____ State_____ Zip_____

Return Offer Certificates to: **PASSPORT TO ROMANCE**, P.O. Box 9057, Buffalo, NY 14269-9057

Requests must be postmarked by **January 25, 1991**

✂

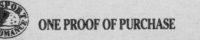

ONE PROOF OF PURCHASE

3-HRG-3

To collect your free coupon booklet you must include the necessary number of proofs-of-purchase with a properly completed Offer Certificate

© 1990 Harlequin Enterprises Limited

See previous page for details